MW01240464

Orange

S. W. Gunn

Orange© 2019 by S.W. Gunn

Design by S.W. Gunn
Cover by Christian Neumann and S.W. Gunn

Print ISBN 979-8-9882511-0-1
Digital ISBN None

FIRST EDITION 2023

To my dragon loving son, Spencer Gunn!

Chapter 1

A loud bellowing came from the left of Rone. He glanced over and spotted another frothing green-skinned orc with a massive club heading towards him. The beasts were simple brutes who were much stronger than Rone or his men, but superior tactics and weapons always won the day.

Rone stood in the middle of the formation and called out the command, "Ready the spears!"

His men formed an impenetrable square with their shields and prepared a row of spears. He grinned. Rone's men were highly trained, and their shoulder high shields would block out any attack, especially once the other men placed their shields around the formation to form an armored square for the first three rows on all sides. The screaming of the orcs echoed in his ears as they slammed into the formation. In order to hold them men in place, several others would hold the ground and brace the primary shield bearers.

"Strike!"

The men in the third row slipped their spears through the notches on the sides of each shield to stab out at the horde of orcs slammed into their wall. Rone checked their flanks to make sure that the bowmen were holding the orcs at bay from climbing over the rough sides of the mountain to cut down on his men. He purposely picked this narrow pass as a pinching point to funnel the orcs right into his formation. It was a tried-and-true strategy when fighting orcs. Against the goblins they would occasionally fight, he had to rely on aggression instead of defense. The goblins were too small and quick for the bowmen to keep them in line.

They were a huge nuisance to deal with. He spotted some orcs trying to climb off to the side and overwhelm his flank.

Yelling loudly at the bowmen Rone said, "Arrows on the left!"

He glanced to the side and watched as the bowmen sent off a volley into the orcs that were climbing up the mountainside. The arrows ripped through them, and they stumbled before falling down the mountainside. He grinned lightly. The battle was going well but Rone know things could shift easily enough. From his standpoint he could see deep into the ranks of their foes. Paying close attention, he spotted orc bowmen lining up to fire into his ranks.

Bellowing out loudly, "Center shields up!"

He lifted his rectangular shield upwards and locked it into place with the other men in his ranks. They would form a box of shields around and over them to protect their ranks in battle. The sounds of arrows thumping roughly against his shield echoed in his ears. He could see a few points from the arrows embedded into his shield as he glanced upwards. Orcs were highly predictable so once the barrage stopped, he lowered his shield. Orcs rarely had just enough arrows to launch one volley. History was proven correct when he examined their line and saw the orcs were again charging.

"Shields down!" He yelled.

The men put their shields down and broke off the arrows embedded into them. He did the same quickly with his gladius.

"Spears readied!" Rone ordered.

His men prepared their spears in the third rank. It was a command to let the men know a charge was coming so they braced themselves. As the orcs once against bashed into his line, the men in the third rank again stabbed out through the shield slots and many orcs fell. At this point the orcs must have realized that they would not break his line so they began to retreat. Rone measured the number of orcs against the number of men he had available. Many times he would call for a sweeping charge to

2

finish his foe but he felt the number of orcs left could overwhelm his men so he decided to let them flee.

The Leftenant approached him and asked, "No charge?"

"No sir. The number of orcs left was too many. We put the hurt to them and outside of a few arrows striking some of our men, we have no injuries."

The Leftenant nodded at him. While technically the Leftenant was the Commanding Officer of the platoon, Rone was the senior Non-Commissioned Officer with seven years of service in the military. At 22 years old, he was the youngest Staff Sergeant in the military, but he was highly seasoned. He joined at 15 when his father was killed by orcs during a raid of his village. Rone was deeply respected and had been awarded the highest military decoration given to anyone in the military, the Golden Cross, during combat two years ago. The Leftenant had been in the military for about a year, and he learned quickly to trust Rone. Teaching the future troops about the military was a large part of his job but also making sure that the Leftenant learned everything he would need to know when he was eventually transferred to a new unit. Rumor had it that Rone himself was going to be up for a possible promotion to First Sergeant again. He was very unsure if that was something he wanted to do. Leading men in battle was in his blood and First Sergeants managed troops back in the barracks. Rone chuckled. That was not the only change threatening his lifestyle, his mother was harassing him every time she saw him to get married. He was the oldest son and she expected him to give her some grandchildren. He just did not feel ready for that and had to reject several proposals his mother made with women back in their village. Arranged marriage was not something he was looking for.

Calling out loudly, he said, "Form up!"

His men moved quickly to form into a square marching formation with their shields and spears on their backs. He grinned at the efficiency of his men. Standing in front of the formation was his senior Sergeant, Makai Harbine.

Rone confidently strode up to the man, who spun towards him and saluted before saying, "Sergeant, the men are ready for your command."

Rone returned the salute before saying, "Thank you Sergeant."

After the Sergeant jogged to the back of the formation Rone stated clearly and loudly, "Men, fine work defending the point. You put a firm whooping on the beasts!"

The men cheered at his declaration. Rone found leading with a firm but reinforcing hand was always the best way to guide his men.

Once the men stopped cheering Rone ordered, "Sergeant, march the formation back to Durnovaria!"

Sergeant Harbine moved directly in front of the formation and saluted Rone again. Rone returned the salute and then strode back over next to the Leftenant.

"Short speech, Sergeant." The Leftenant commented.

"Yes sir. I didn't want the orcs returning midway through a rousing speech."

The Leftenant chuckled. Rone nodded. The Leftenant removed his helmet, which was something Rone had always told the men never to do while in the mountains. Orc bowmen could shoot your head.

"Sir, please put your helmet back on. It's not safe out here."

The Leftenant did not say a word but put his helmet on. The man had brown hair and brown eyes. It contrasted Rone's own light blonde hair and sharp blue eyes. He was also a bit smaller than Rone, who was a tiny bit over 18 hands tall. He was the second tallest man in the formation and between his experience and size, he was highly respected by his men. The weather was a lovely spring day with the sun shining brightly in the early morning. The air was crisp, and the smell of victory made things even sweeter. All of his men would survive, the few injured men would need a few weeks' rest but they would be back on the front again soon. He was about to get a nice three-day break, along with his men, to wait for their next orders. The Sharp Talon Platoon was one of the most battle ready and experienced platoons in the entire military. He was its senior Non-Commissioned Officer. The formation marched down on the rough mountain pathway without issue and it was not long until they made their way back to the barracks.

Once they got to the barracks the Leftenant said, "Sergeant, I'm going to report the results of our successful battle to the Colonel. Release the men for their break and stand fast until I return."

"Yes sir."

Rone watched the Leftenant walk away before turning to release the men. He then went to the hospice to ensure the injured men were looked after. Each man was quite pleased to see him arrive and he made sure to let them know their spots within the platoon were secure. He was very happy that none of them were seriously injured. Most of his troops were young men who had much to live for in their future. The world was harsh, so men had to iron themselves to the world early. Orcs, goblins, undead, and plenty of other monsters threatened to kill them all so Rone and his men held the path. When Durnovaria was nothing but a small village, it struggled to hold the path and many times men and women suffered. Now, it was a sprawling town with dozens of small villages under its protection. His men came from Durnovaria and many of the nearby villages. He was proud of his service and would probably continue to serve until he could no longer do so. Strolling back to the Leftenant's office, which was attached to their barrack's building, he spotted the Leftenant in the distance walking towards the barracks. He was carrying a leather-wrapped package.

As the Leftenant approached he saluted Rone and then said, "The Colonel was quite pleased with the results of our battle."

Rone saluted back as he stated, "Excellent news sir."

"Come in my office Sergeant."

"Yes sir."

Rone followed closely behind the Leftenant and then sat down in the open chair across the Leftenant's desk as the man sat down.

"Sergeant Millar, you have done an outstanding job leading our men and I've been honored to serve with you."

"Thank you sir."

Rone was puzzled. The Leftenant sounded slightly upset as though something Rone was unaware of happened.

The man continued, "I've been transferred to serve within General Taylor's staff and in a few days the new Leftenant will be arriving."

Rone nodded. Transfers were common within the officer ranks. This Leftenant was actually from the capital city of Ironania and he had only been here for a while. Many times these officers showed up to learn combat and the basics of being in the military in units like Rone's. It was the enlisted who they tended to keep within the area in which they were from. It helped keep motivation high if a man was defending his own home.

Rone told the man, "It's been an honor serving with you Leftenant."

The Leftenant responded, "It has indeed. I've learned more from my time with you as my Sergeant than any other assignment. I have to admit that I didn't want this transfer but the Colonel insisted that he had to push as many new officers through your Platoon as he could so they'd learn from you. There aren't too many living Golden Cross awardees."

Rone blushed. While it was an honor to receive the Golden Cross, the burdens of it sometimes became frustrating to deal with. Officers saluting him, the men treating him more like some sort of mythical character, and it set a standard he many times feared he could never meet. The Leftenant stood and extended a hand. Rone clasped the man's hand.

Once he released his grasp the Leftenant stated, "The Colonel asked me to have you deliver this package for him."

"I'll get a Private to deliver it immediately sir."

"No." The Leftenant responded.

"No?" Rone asked.

"It's a priority delivery for the General and he personally asked that you deliver it."

Rone raised an eyebrow. Usually, these sorts of menial tasks were best performed by the junior enlisted.

Realizing that there must have been something important about the package he shrugged and said, "I'll take it immediately. Where am I delivering it to?"

"There's a small village called Conberry at the edges of the farmlands to the north-east of Durnovaria."

"I know it sir."

"It's the General's dress tabard and he wants you to bring it to a seamstress there for repairs."

Rone frowned. This task was very much below something he should personally dealing with. It seemed like an argument not worth fighting so he picked up the package.

"I'll find it."

"Drop it off and then pick it back up and deliver it once the seamstress is done."

This was unfortunate. It sounded like Rone's three free days off were about to be occupied by waiting for this tabard.

The Leftenant saluted him and stated, "Dismissed Sergeant."

Returning the salute Rone said, "Yes sir."

Chapter 2

Tucking the package that was handed to him into a saddlebag, Rone mounted his pinto-colored horse and started to head off. He was pretty confused as to why the General wanted him personally to be a delivery boy but he figured that it was not going to hurt anything to just deliver this package. At least the ride would be a pleasant one. The weather was still lovely and he always did enjoy a nice ride through the open fields around town. Surrounding Durnovaria was a heavy wooden wall. It was meant to keep the enemies of the Kingdom within the mountains at bay if they ever managed to get through the military forces that patrolled the nearby mountainside. The walls only had 4 gates, one to each cardinal direction. Each was heavily manned by a platoon of men. When Rone first joined he was assigned to the East gate and had worked his way up to where he was now. He chose to exit out of the East gate merely for sentimental purposes. He had manned the two posts set on top of the gates there many times.

As he passed through the gate he heard the Captain of the Guard called out, "Attention."

Rone raised his hand in salute of the man. Even the General was required to salute Rone. He found it very embarrassing but he would always follow regulation. His horse slowly clopped along. Rone took a deep breath and enjoyed the crisp air. It was slowly closing in on lunch time. It had been a long time since he had been to Conberry but if he remembered correctly it was a pleasant little farming village. He only brought his gladius with him, as per regulations, while technically on a mission. Outside the town were rolling fields of farmlands.

Everything from grains to vegetables were grown in these fields. Durnovaria was the breadbasket of the Kingdom, which is why there was such a strong military force here. He loved his homeland quite a bit. After about an hour of riding, he saw the village in the distance that he was heading to. It looked exactly the same as the last time he had been there, about three years ago. Unlike Durnovaria, the villages did not have walls around them. He spotted about twenty or so buildings, with none of them being more than a single story in height. The roads were cobbled with smooth stone, just like the rest of the Kingdom. There was an aqueduct and funneled slots along the stone roads to keep people's chamber pots from making the villages stink. As he entered the village, he spotted several dozen men and women walking around. It seemed odd to him that most of the people were older. Maybe this was one of those villages with very few young people staying because many would leave for Durnovaria. Most that caught his eye and would give him a polite wave. He always responded with a wave back. Unlike bigger towns like Durnovaria, these villages tended to be friendlier to strangers. It reminded him of his own home village where his family still lived.

Wanting to know where the seamstress was he stopped and asked an elderly man wearing a simple off-white tunic, tan trousers, and wrapped sandals, "Sir could you please direct me to the seamstress?"

Rubbing his chin, the man responded, "The Taylors. They're living at the northern part of the village in a building with two flowing banners that had a spindle emblazoned on it."

Waving at the man Rone said, "Thank you sir."

Rone turned his horse north towards where the man directed him. He waved at several more people as he went. Finally, he spotted the building in question. It was made of the same simple concrete that many other homes were built of. Hanging off the front of the building were two banners with a spindle on it. This was clearly the location in question. He dismounted his horse and tied its reins to the small stand in front of the building. He heard a light female voice giggling at something inside the building. He could not hear what was being said that caused her to respond that way. Digging into his saddlebag, he pulled out the leather package. The door to the home was not one simple door but two doors that were nicely decorated with a detailed etching along the sides that circled around and met at the dividing point of the two doors. He wondered how a seamstress in a small village could afford the craftsmanship needed for such a fine looking door. Hanging on the door was a sign that said, 'Open'. Reaching out, he opened the door and stepped in. The first thing he noticed entering was the smell of some kind of flower. No doubt it was coming from burning incense. The room was well lit with a long wide-open counter that had needles, cloth, thread, and a bunch of materials no doubt used to make or repair clothing. He had no idea what any of them were. As he slowly examined the room his eyes froze, and he was immediately drawn in on the woman who was obviously the source of the laughing that he had heard. She was maybe around 18 years old. Her bright orange hair was braided into two thick braids and pinned onto the back of her head. She had almost white skin, a delicate looking face, and light brown eyes. She was wearing a flowing light green full length dress that was stitched with golden thread throughout it that did not form a specific pattern. For some reason she was staring directly at him, and their eyes locked onto each other right away. She was simply quite lovely to him. Women with her hair color were quite rare in most of the Kingdom but near Durnovaria it was more common.

Another, male, voice grumpily asked, "Can we help you."

It shook him out of his moment of pause so he brought the package up and set it on the counter before saying, "Yes sorry, the General asked me to bring his tabard for repairs."

He glanced toward the voice that had spoken to see that it was a massive light skinned man with bright orange hair that was tied back into a single braid. He had the same color eyes as the woman and was very likely, and hopefully, a relative. He was wearing a dark brown tunic, black trousers, and a pair of wrapped sandals.

Clapping her hands excitedly, "Oh Uncle Gerrard sent him with it."

Rone raised his eyebrow at her and asked, "Gerrard?"

"Your General is my uncle and Henri's father." She answered gesturing at the large man.

"Oh," Rone responded before he commented, "I guess it'd make sense to send his tabard for repairs to someone that he trusts."

A piece of him was glad to hear that the large man was her cousin.

He found her voice absolutely lyrical as she responded, "It does. What's your name?"

"Rone Millar."

"A strong name."

"Thank you."

"So… let's see what Uncle Gerrard wants fixed up."

She opened the package. Rone watched her intently. She was petite and stood about a hand and a half or so shorter than he was. He had not noticed initially but she had a splattering of freckles on her face and her hands, likely she was covered in them. She opened the package to reveal the tabard in question. It was like every other general's tabard made in wine red color with gold lining. Upon the breast was a golden seven-pointed star, the symbol of a general. As she moved it, she found a long tear along the seams. It looked as though someone had roughly pulled the tabard apart and he wondered how the world a General would have his tabard torn in such a manner. He examined her hands closely and saw no jewelry.

Direly wanting to know her name he asked, "What's your name?"

She looked at him and answered, "Marah Taylor."

He grinned at her answer. Her name was just as pretty as she was. She smiled back before flushing lightly and looking back at the tabard. He desperately wanted to learn more about her but he was hit by a sudden and very strong sense of nervousness. Rone had fought down hordes of monsters, but he was not sure how or if it was appropriate to ask a lady questions about her without offending. He scratched his scraggly light blonde beard that he had started to grow about a month ago. It was not very impressive yet, but he felt that it would make him older and more mature looking.

She finished playing with the tabard before announcing, "It will take me a day to fix it. It looks like something pulled it apart but I'm pretty good at fixing almost anything."

Rone nodded at her before saying, "That's good to know. I'm certain that the General knew you could, or he'd have not sent it here."

She looked right at him again as she asked, "Will you be the one picking it up?"

"I will."

Clapping her hands together joyfully she said, "I'm glad to hear it. Is there anything else I can do for you Rone?"

"No Marah. I was just sent here to bring the General's tabard."

"A shame." She replied with a little smile.

"Marah." The large man, who she said was her cousin said in a stern tone.

"What?" She said to the man in response.

"Behave. The Sergeant is here for work."

"I just said. Look at his uniform. It's so shiny. I've never seen the gold lining along the collar and sleeves like that. Maybe he needed someone to fit it or some other thing he needed work on."

Rone chuckled. She was quite a peppy young lady as well as pretty. He would have liked to get to know her better but he was not sure flirting with the General's niece was a very wise life choice.

Rejecting his own thoughts, he asked, "What time tomorrow shall I return?"

Marah looked back over him and answered, "About noon. I should have it looking perfect by then."

"Okay. It was a pleasure meeting the both of you."

Marah smiled widely at him and replied, "It has been a pleasure meeting you too Rone."

He grinned and waved awkwardly at her before stepping out the two doors. As he mounted is horse he realized that he was quite excited about coming back tomorrow to pick up the tabard. This mission went from a dreadful waste of his time to something he was happy about quite quickly. His mind began to wonder about how he could find a way to court her. She was so lovely, and he was immediately drawn to her cheery personality. He could see the little twinkle in her eye as she spoke and for some reason he had convinced himself that she was attracted to him. A large part of him felt that he was probably seeing something that was not there out of hope, after all she was in the business of providing a service to customers so being kind was a requirement. He also wondered how angry the General would have if Rone tried to see her outside of this little mission. The General was the man who presented the Golden Cross award to Rone and while he seemed polite enough, the man was very stern looking. Thinking about it, the General did look like a much older version than her cousin, Henri. They were both very large men, which was uncommon. Rone was considered big, and they both made him look normal in size. Tapping the sides of his horse he headed off. Looking over his shoulder back at the building that Marah was in, he saw the door close. He did not see who closed it but it was odd. Shrugging he turned back around and headed off.

Chapter 3

Light cracking through the window of Rone's private quarters, forcing him to wake up. He was thankful of his position in the military since it meant that he was allowed private quarters away from the barracks and his men. He struggled sleeping last night due to his mind's sudden preoccupation with the seamstress niece of the General. Daydreams about taking her out on a date and then general ordering him flogged tossed through his head. Peering out his window, after he stood up, he saw that it was still a few hours before he had to be back to her shop to pick up the tabard. He was quite excited for the prospect since he would be able to see Marah again. Since he had time, he decided to visit the bathing house and clean up before getting breakfast. He made sure to bring his uniform so he could leave right after finishing up. Marah also seemed to like his uniform so he was more than willing to wear it.

As he stepped out of the bathing house in his uniform a nearby soldier said, "Good morning Sergeant."

Rone looked at the man. He was not a member of his platoon and was in uniform. He was a young man with trimmed blonde hair, blue eyes, and clean shaven. His uniform tunic was a duller wine red color and he had the rank stripes on his collar for a Private. He saluted Rone.

Grinning at the man, Rone saluted and then replied, "Good morning Private."

Rone made his way to the dining hall that served as the only place military men were allowed to eat their meals for free. If they wished to eat anything else they would have to pay, like any other citizen. The dining hall was serving plenty of options so he took some bread with wine for dipping, some olives, and a few slices of cheese. It was his usual choice for breakfast since he liked to keep it simple. After eating he had to greet and salute a few more soldiers before he mounted his horse and headed off. His mind kept going back to thinking about the General's niece. A wave of nervousness hit him when he realized that he was about to see her again. It was a feeling about a woman he had not had in a long time, usually his career in the military was his singular focus. While he had no idea why the General picked him specifically for this task, he was thanking the gods for it. Since it was still his favorite gate, he went through the East gate again.

As it had been each time, he heard the Captain of the Guard called out, "Attention."

Rone saluted back and continued riding his horse through the gate. It was another beautiful spring day and Rone really enjoyed it. He doubted that even if it was raining or even snowing that his mood would have been dampened. It was a little bit over an hour before he made it back to the village that he was going to came into view. His nerves began to build again. Several people greeted him as he rode through the village. He turned up the road and headed to the building where Marah worked. Once he arrived, he dismounted and tied his horse up to the small stand there. Rone stopped right at the door and took a deep breath to try and calm his nerves. He could not fathom exactly why he was so nervous about seeing a woman he did not know. Steeling himself he boldly reached out and opened the door before stepping in. The room looked exactly the same with the only real difference being the incense being burned seemed to be some kind of wood instead of a flower scent.

"Welcome back Rone!" Marah said with a tone of voice that sounded happy.

Almost on reflex he replied, "Thank you."

His mind twisted once again thinking that she liked him fighting against the idea that she was just being polite to a customer. He took her in and noted that she had completely changed her hairstyle to a be loosely wrapped into a neat bun on

15

the back of her head. She was wearing a much more form fitting blue dress that had a swirling pattern of different shaped white flowers all over it. Her sleeves were pulled up past her elbows as she was leaning over the counter while diligently working on the tabard that he had brought her yesterday.

She announced, "I'm not done with the tabard yet. Please feel free to take a seat on a stool and wait."

He nodded at her and pulled a stool to sit down up against her counter, opposite her. Her brow was furrowed in deep concentration as she worked a needle attached to some thread through the fabric of the tabard. Maybe it was his imagination but she was even prettier seeing her again than he swore she was the day before.

While she was working she asked, "So how was your evening?"

He was mildly surprised by the question so he paused for a moment before answering, "It was fine. I went back to the barracks and double checked on my men before I had supper and then retired for the evening."

"So… no family?" She asked.

"My father was killed by an orc attack and my mother lives in Peel, same with my siblings. I'm the oldest."

She nodded solemnly while she continued to slowly work on the tabard.

"How long have you been in the military?"

He told her, "A bit over seven years."

"Whoa… you look much younger than you must be if you've been in the military for 7 years."

"I'm twenty-two years old. I joined when I was fifteen."

"Ahhh… my mistake, why did you join so young?"

"Because I was upset that my father was murdered by orcs."

She frowned as she said, "I'm sorry."

"It's okay Marah. It was long ago."

"Do you regret it?"

"No. I love what I do." He honestly told her.

16

"I'm seventeen."

Rone frowned. If she was seventeen, he highly doubted that she was interested in being courted by a man looking for a possible wife.

She must have seen his frown because she asked, "Is that bad?"

He quickly lied since he did not want to push her away, "No… No. I just was thinking about something in my platoon."

She looked up at him and saw that he was watching her. Their eyes met again, and she smiled at him. He returned her smile. Marah blushed for some reason before she turned back to her work.

Wanting to learn about her and figuring that since she asked him questions, she would not mind him asking her a few things so he asked, "What about your family?"

She kept working as she answered, "I was adopted by Uncle Gerrard when I was six."

He nodded. Orphans were quite common in the Kingdom, especially here when dealing with the many monsters that would attack the villages. The orphanage was almost always full and she was quite lucky to have been adopted.

"I didn't ask, how was your evening?" He asked.

Looking up at him again she grinned and then answered, "I had three orders that I finished, then I went to Durnovaria with my family to visit Uncle Gerrard."

Rone found it unusual that he was sent to deliver the tabard when his family came to see him there.

She continued speaking, "We usually don't go to see him there but Auntie wanted to surprise him with some homemade cream buns. I've only been to town a few times, so it was quite exciting."

He nodded. That made much more sense. It was a good thing she was concentrating so hard on sewing the tabard because it allowed him the opportunity to look at her without being embarrassed by her noticing.

There was a long moment of silence before she asked, "What is your rank?"

"Staff Sergeant." He answered.

She nodded at his answer, but he could tell instantly from her facial expression she did not know what it meant. Really, it probably did not matter when your uncle was the General in command of all of the forces in the area. Likely her uncle was the reason the doors were so nice and the clothing she wore was as fancy as it was. The Generals in the military were paid quite well. His pay was nowhere on the level of the General, but he was paid well enough and since he had very few expenses he had saved much of it. The only exception was a small stipend of his pay that he sent to help support his widowed mother. Marah finished her work and then cut off the stitching before gently folding the tabard and placing it back in the leather package. She passed it over to him.

"Thank you." He told her.

"That will be two silver pieces." She told him.

He was surprised. The idea that he would have to pay for the General's repairs to his own family had not crossed his mind. He stumbled for a moment to dig out his coin purse.

She giggled at him before saying, "I'm just playing Rone."

He chuckled at her. She was indeed playful, and he liked it. Picking up the package he stood up.

"Thank you." He told her.

"Of course." She replied with a soft smile.

He gave her a grin before turning and heading towards the door.

As he opened the door Marah said to him, "If you need any other work please remember me."

Looking back, he said, "I will."

While moving through the door Marah said very softly, which he was certain she did not mean for him to hear, "I hope you come back soon."

18

It was a pleasant visit and he was certain that she was indeed interested in him. Deciding that he needed to talk to his mother for advice, he mounted his horse and rode off. It was only an hour-long ride to the west where his mother lived in Peel. The whole ride he spent thinking about his interaction with Marah. Her last attempted comment was all he needed. His only concern was how he would see things through. His mother would be the one who could help him. As he entered Peel, he rode slightly to the north. His family were farmers who grew wheat and milled it for sale. They made some of the best flour in the Kingdom. Two of his younger brothers were adults and had split his father's land in half for work. Rone passed his rights to the land to his brothers so he could serve in the military. They supported their mother and their younger siblings. He dismounted and tied his horse to a stand by the door. Their home was made of the same concrete as most homes in the Kingdom but its single wooden door was much simpler than Marah's.

As he stepped into the home he called out, "Mother!"

"Rone?" Her voice responded back.

"Yes mother. I've come for a visit."

He had 2 sisters and a very young little brother who still were not adults and lived with his mother. Only seven years old, his little brother loved him and came racing when Rone spoke.

Giving the little man a hug Rone said, "It's nice to see you again Mavin."

"Rone, did you kill some more orcs today?"

Chuckling at the boy Rone answered, "No. I'm fighting another thing today."

"What's that Rone?"

"A girl."

"Ewww… Those are worse than orcs." The boy announced before dropping down and taking off.

Rone laughed heartily.

"A girl?" His mother asked as she entered the main room of their home.

Her hair was the same blonde color as his and she had his light blue eyes. He got much of his appearance from her. She was wearing a simple loose fitting brown dress with a tan leather belt wrapped around her waist.

Blushing heavily Rone answered, "I was sent to deliver something for the General and there was a young woman who works as a seamstress there. I think she's quite lovely and she was very friendly with me."

His mother nodded before asking, "And you want to court her?"

"I do but I've got some concerns."

She raised an eyebrow as she asked, "Which are?"

"She's the niece of the General in question."

"Do you think she likes you?"

He nodded as he responded, "I don't know for certain since a lady does not push herself on a man she isn't being courted by but she did whisper something as I was leaving that I believe she did not mean for me to hear."

"And it was?"

He grinned while saying, "She said she hoped I would come back."

"How old is she?"

"Seventeen."

His mother nodded and paused to look thoughtful for a moment before finally saying, "I don't know why the fact she is the niece of this general is a problem."

"What if he doesn't want a military man dating his niece?"

Laughing his mother asked, "What was the status of this tabard you delivered?"

He was confused why his mother suddenly started laughing but he answered, "It was torn along the seam on the right side."

She laughed even harder and eventually after calming down she announced to him, "Son, you're a brave soldier and a good looking young man but you're being set up."

"Set up?" He asked rubbing his chin.

He was very confused.

"This General picked you for a silly delivery because he wants you court his niece."

"You think so?"

"Why in the world would he need to have his torn tabard delivered to his own family otherwise? Think about it. You're a decorated soldier who is young, fit, honorable and good looking. You'd be a perfect choice for any man to match up with young women in his family."

His mother must have been right and he found her words very reassuring.

"Mother what do I do now?"

"Go right up to her father and ask him if you could court his daughter."

"She's adopted by the General."

"Go right up to that general and ask him if you could court her."

"You don't just go right up to the General."

"Yes you do. If you like her, make it happen Rone."

"Yes mother."

"Stay for supper."

Chapter 4

Rone was very disappointed when he made it back to Durnovaria. It turned out that the General had been send to the Capital of the Kingdom for a meeting. Likely something Generals had to do regularly. His hopes of asking to court Marah would have to wait until the General returned. He had to stew on his own thoughts for a day before it was time to get back to the Platoon. Today he was going to meet the new Leftenant and then they would get their next assignment. Rone got ready for his day and headed off to the Leftenant's office. It made sense that the new Leftenant would report there first. As he walked to the office he spotted a young man standing outside the office. He was a little bit shorter than Rone with cropped brown hair, brown eyes, and a slightly patchy brown beard. Rone guessed that he was likely the same age as Rone. He was wearing a military wine red tunic and black trousers with wrapped sandals. The collar of his tunic had the marks for a Leftenant. This man was definitely the new Leftenant.

As Rone approached, the man asked, "Sergeant Rone Millar?"

"Yes sir." Rone answered while nodding at the man.

The new Leftenant then asked, "Is it not tradition for enlisted men to salute their new Officer in Charge?"

Not wanting to embarrass the man in public Rone responded, "Sir, let's go in your office to talk about it."

Rone gestured towards the office door. The new Leftenant turned and walked through the door. Rone followed him in.

As the Leftenant sat down Rone said, "Sir. I know you're new to the Platoon so I wanted to"

The Leftenant cut him off by declaring, "I'm the Officer in Charge of this Platoon and I'm expecting you to always perform all customs and courtesies due me."

Rone was not surprised by the man's curtness. Many times newer Officers missed little details in their aim to take charge and be the man running things. It was important for the Officer in Charge and Non-Commissioned Officer in Charge to have a smooth relationship so Rone always had to be careful. Many Officers were selected not on their talent but because of their family's importance.

Nodding at the man Rone said, "Of course sir. I didn't salute you because I'm an awardee of the Golden Cross."

The man looked thoughtful for a moment before he finally said, "Oh. I was wondering why my instructor back in Officer's Education was so excited when I told him I was selected for this assignment."

Rone grinned before stating, "Personally it was a great honor but it can be a burden at times, especially with the younger soldiers. I'm excited to show you the ropes and get you up to speed. Just remember sir, I'm here to help you become the best Officer you can be. Every Leftenant who I've served with us has gone onto great things. No doubt you were selected for this post because you have vast potential."

"Thank you Sergeant. I've received orders that we're to take a scouting team southeast of the southern gate to locate an enemy village."

Rone chuckled. It was likely another attempt to find the village that the orcs who kept trying to attack outposts near the southern gate lived at. He had been on more than his share of these scouting missions. They find a village and send a large force to deal with it. Usually the orcs in these villages tended to be women and children so they run right away when met with a large force. He had to admit that he was more than a little wary about killing women and children, even monsters like orcs. Many times

Rone wondered how exactly war started between men and these creatures. He knew that they were sentient, although it seemed to barely be the case.

"Sounds like a plan sir. Usually we go with a small and mobile force that can weave through the mountainside and retreat quickly if needed."

The Leftenant nodded. He was clearly mulling over Rone's suggestion.

"Horseback?" The Leftenant asked.

"Sadly not once we get past the first third of the mountain. We usually set them in a spot with a large group of guards and reinforcement while the main scouting force moves on foot. Horses tend to be very loud when attempting to scout and the orcs have sharp hearing."

"Oh. I guess they aren't mindless brutes?"

"Honestly sir, they aren't the smartest but they have many abilities that make them hard to deal with."

"Such as?"

"They breed rapidly, they can see in the dark, they are much stronger than we are, and they are fearless. Many times our men have cowered at the sight of a charging horde."

The Leftenant thoughtfully rubbed his chin before asking, "Who should I select for this mission?"

"We've got a selection of men who are more skilled at stealth than most that I usually suggest. I'd like you to accompany them as it would be an excellent opportunity for you to get to know the men you'll be leading."

"I'm excited for the opportunity Sergeant."

"Yes sir. Shall we?"

The Leftenant nodded at him. Rone led him out of the office and into the barracks.

As soon as Rone entered the barracks he yelled out, "Attention!"

His men raced from loitering around to standing in position near their bunks.

24

Rone said loudly, "Soldiers. Let me introduce you boys to the new Leftenant."

The men called out, "Good morning sir!"

The Leftenant said, "Good morning soldiers. I'm excited to serve with the best platoon in the Kingdom!"

The men cheered loudly. Once they calmed down slightly the Leftenant gestured with his hand, which silenced the men.

"I have high standards and I have the highest confidence in each of you to execute. Today we've got a scouting mission. Sergeant…"

Rone nodded at the Leftenant before saying, "Scout team 2, Sergeant Clarke you'll take the lead on this with the Leftenant and I on this mission."

Sergeant Clarke, a shorter man with tanned skin, brown hair, and brown eyes, said, "Yes Sergeant. The usual gear Sergeant?"

"Of course. Light and fast. Be ready in 20 minutes."

"Yes Sergeant!"

Rone nodded and then grinned at the Leftenant. The Leftenant turned and exited the barracks.   Someone yelled, "Attention!"

As Rone stepped out the Leftenant asked, "Sergeant, what will I need for this mission?"

"A horse, a sword, and the ability to be really quiet. Oh, and if they spot us, the ability to run as fast as you can." Rone answered with a light chuckle.

"Easy enough."

Rone nodded. The Leftenant excused himself and after a few moments returned with a sword strapped around his waist. It was a standard military issued gladius. Sergeant Clarke and Scout team 2 came out of the barracks and formed up. They were ready to go. The Leftenant looked over at Rone. Rone nodded at him to let him know to take charge.

The Leftenant announced, "Sergeant Clarke, this is your show. Sergeant Millar and I will follow along with you."

"Yes sir." Sergeant Clarke said before ordering the men, "Mount up!"

Rone mounted his horse along with the men and followed them as they rode out of the southern gate. It was a brief ride through the mountainside before they turned off towards the east. The last few sightings of orcs were to the east so that is where they would likely find the village. The weather was lightly drizzling rain but otherwise it was warm and pleasant. Rone smiled to himself. His mother's words about the General setting him up to court his niece pleased him greatly. She was lovely looking, charming, and obviously liked him. Daydreaming about spending time with her excited him. He decided that their first date would be a picnic. Something simple and in the open since he wanted to let her and her family know that he was an honorable man. He only dreaded approaching the General about it but if his mother said it would be fine, he knew it would be fine. His mother was always right.

"Halt!" Sergeant Clarke ordered.

Rone blinked. He was daydreaming about Marah the whole ride and did not even notice that they had arrived at the guard location. Here they would leave the horses and move on foot towards the direction orcs were last seen moving by other scout teams. Rone dismounted and strolled over to Sergeant Clarke. He was mostly there to supervise the Leftenant than the Scout team. Normally he would run these types of missions from back in town and trust his senior Non-commissioned Officers to execute things. His soldiers have been doing this for years and had absolute trust in each other.

"How far will we walk?" The Leftenant asked.

Sergeant Clarke answered, "Sir, maybe three or four leagues and then we'll come back if we don't spot any orcs. Private Armstrong will track location in case we spot them for the reports."

The Leftenant nodded at him.

"From here out, hand signals only." Sergeant Clarke ordered.

Rone followed behind the soldiers as they slowly began walking. Private Grant took the lead and was several paces in front of the whole group. They drew their swords. It was important to be ready to fight if needed. Rone drew his sword as well. His men walked smoothly and silently as they went. He was proud of them. They were highly trained at scouting and executed near perfectly. Grant waved from in front of them and then put up three fingers before waving at himself. He knelt. It was the symbol for leadership to silently approach. Rone gestured with his head quietly at the Leftenant to follow. The man nodded at him as they slowly crept up to Grant with Sergeant Clarke. Once they all arrived at the point where Grant was kneeling, Grant gestured with a hand in front of him. Rone looked there and spotted a rough looking dirty village. They had found the village in question. Based on the number of orcs that Rone saw, he doubted it was the main village but a smaller one. It was filled mostly with women and children; he saw only a few male orcs. The creatures lived a crude lifestyle that reminded Rone of the history of the Kingdom from centuries ago. These orcs were wearing furs covering their body and used sticks or rocks for their few tools. He spotted a few elderly orcs, which was something he had never seen before. Rone assumed that they did not live long lives due to their violent nature. Realizing that attacking this village would be a waste of military resources, Rone gestured a closing movement with his hand. He wanted them to withdraw to a range where they could discuss things.

They followed Rone as he withdrew and they silently walked far enough away to talk Rone asked, "Sir, what do you think?"

He wanted to get a gauge on the morality and intellect of the new Leftenant.

The Leftenant answered, "It seemed as though it was women, children, and old creatures only."

Rone nodded.

"We must report our findings to Command and let them decide how to act."

Rubbing his chin, Rone commented, "Usually Command appreciates a recommendation within the assessment since we have firsthand knowledge of the level of threat. What should we say sir?"

The Leftenant looked thoughtful for a moment before answered, "I wouldn't put a high level of threat on this village but regulation would call for its elimination."

New Officers tended to lead by regulation first and it took some time in the field and with men dealing with the issues at hand personally for them to think outside basic regulation.

"What do you think Sergeant?" The Leftenant asked.

Rone nodded at him before answering, "I'd report the village but put no threat value and recommend not to waste military resources on it."

"Why?" The Leftenant asked.

In his most serious tone that Rone could bring himself to say, "Sir, let me ask you an honest question."

"Go ahead."

"Do you want to be the one to kill them?"

The Leftenant frowned. Few men wanted to kill women and children, even if those women and children were enemies. It was considered less than honorable to do so and Rone refused to do so. It had caused him issue with Command only one time in his career and after he was awarded the Golden Cross he was never challenged on his decisions again.

After a very long pause the Leftenant answered, "I would not."

Rone grinned at him before saying, "No man of honor would. Either we report this village and state it isn't worth the military's effort or we don't report it at all. At least that is what I suggest sir. I'll support your report however you wish to write it."

"Thank you Sergeant."

Sergeant Clarke announced, "We've marked their position and its time to head back to town."

After the Leftenant nodded at Sergeant Clarke they headed off. It was a bit of a walk back to their horses and then a thankfully brief ride to town. They would make it back in time for supper. Rone was hoping for the General's return so he could conclude his own personal business very soon. After a nice walk they made it to their horses and mounted up. Rone made sure to follow behind his men as they rode towards town. As soon as they headed down the mountainside they were passing a group of trees. The Leftenant brushed a large branch away from himself and it kicked back into Rone. Leaning to his left he avoided the branch but felt it tug against his right tunic sleeve. It pulled roughly before he jerked his arm free. Once he cleared the branch he looked down at his tunic and saw that the branch had somehow snagged his tunic and pulled the gold edging off the sleeve. It was not hanging loosely.

"Dang it." He muttered out.

The Leftenant looked back at him. Rone gestured at the torn edging of his sleeve. The Leftenant nodded and turned back. Rone was suddenly struck with the realization that he now had a very convenient excuse to visit Marah. It made him laugh heartily.

Chapter 5

Rone paced back and forth in the waiting room of the General's office. The General returned two days after Rone's platoon finished the scouting mission. Rone was pleased that the new Leftenant seemed flexible in dealing with missions. His report about the village stated that it was a low threat and military effort would be a waste of resources. Today Rone wanted the Leftenant to spend time with the men without Rone interfering to see how he would do with the men. It also gave Rone an opportunity to speak with the General about Marah. His nerves were at a record high as he had to pace to keep himself from going insane. The waiting room was not very big with only a few chairs for people to sit in. Hanging on the walls were several elegant paintings. It was a fine looking waiting room. The door to the General's office opened and a man stepped out. It was the Major who served as the attaché of the General. He was of average height with light blonde hair that was neatly trimmed, green eyes, and he was clean shaven. Rone guessed that he was probably around forty years old because he did have a few wrinkles on his face. Like all military men, he was wearing a wine-red tunic, black trousers, and the same wrapped sandals that Rone was wearing.

"The General only has a few minutes but he'll see you now." The man stated.

"Yes sir." Rone said.

Taking a deep breath to calm himself Rone followed the Major in. The office of the General was as fancy as Rone imagined that it would be. There was a huge desk made of some type of wood that was polished sitting in the center of the room.

Along the back wall was a wooden bookshelf made of the same type of wood that was filled with a variety of books. Along the walls were several paintings, one of which appeared to be the General himself with his family. Marah was in the painting. There was a soft looking couch along the wall under that painting. In front of the desk was a chair for a guest to sit in and behind the desk was a much larger chair. The General was sitting in that chair. He was exactly how Rone remembered him. He had silvered, almost white, hair that was cut in a military style. His eyes were the same color as Marah's, he had a neatly trimmed beard that matched his silvered hair, and he was wearing the proper military uniform. Over his uniform was the tabard that Rone took to get repaired. He looked less than amused to see Rone, which Rone hoped was due to his busy schedule.

Standing at attention, Rone saluted and then said, "Sir, Staff Sergeant Rone Millar requests permission to speak."

"Speak." The General said sternly.

"Umm… Sir would it be possible to talk privately?"

The General rubbed his chin and then placed it on his hand while resting his elbow on the desk he was sitting at before stating, "This man is my most trusted associate. Do you feel as though what you are about to say is something that a man who listens to secret briefings should not listen to?"

"Sir I… Sir… Well, what I wished to talk to you about was of a personal nature."

"And he's been at my home for some of my most important life events, including my recent 60th birthday celebration."

Taking a moment to calm himself and take a deep breath Rone decided to just go for it.

"Sir, I'd like to… well I was wondering if…"

"Spit it out Sergeant, I don't have all day to listen to you stumble over your words."

"Yes sir. I'd like permission to court your niece Marah."

There was a long pause of silence. Rone was relieved to finally get it out but he was concerned that the General did not seem amused by the request.

The General turned to the Major and asked, "Major, what do you think of the nerve of this Staff Sergeant strolling into my office and requesting permission to court the most angelic young woman in my life?"

Giving a chuckle the Major answered, "It takes some nerve sir. I've known Marah since she was a little girl. She's like a daughter to me almost as much as she is to you."

The General nodded at him.

"Indeed Major, she's the daughter I've never had. I'm curious what this man's intentions are. Likely just looking to roll about in the hay since she's particularly attractive."

Rone frowned. He most certainly was not thinking in such a manner. Sure, he found her to be lovely looking but simply bedding her was not his intent.

Deciding not to tolerate even the General questioning his honor Rone stated firmly, "I don't appreciate my honor being questioned sir. My intentions are gentlemanly."

The General grinned at Rone. Maybe Rone's response is exactly what the General was looking for?

Looking over at the General, the Major stated, "And he's got a spine too. Maybe you should give him a chance sir?"

"You think Major?"

"If I had a vote sir, I'd say give him a chance but have Henri ready just in case a thrashing is needed."

Once again the General slowly ran his hand through his beard. Rone could only wonder what he was thinking about. A small part of Rone regretted even trying but he knew that he liked her and was completely honorable in his purpose. The General's right hand moved away from his beard and then picked up something off his desk. Rone was so nervous he missed the detail of what the General had on his desk. The General then tossed something directly at Rone. Using his own right hand, Rone caught whatever it was that the General threw at him. He glanced down and saw it was the General's coin! The General had given consent! Rone grinned.

"Go ahead Sergeant. Be warned, you break her heart and you'll have me to answer to."

Nodding at the man Rone responded, "Yes sir. I promise my intentions are honorable."

"Dismissed Sergeant."

"Yes sir!"

Rone spun on his heel and headed out. His nervousness was gone and he was now extremely happy. He could hardly contain himself and would go directly to Marah's home to ask her. He only hoped that she agreed to a picnic or he would be greatly embarrassed. Since the men with the Leftenant would not be back until later in the day, Rone decided to head directly to the village where Marah lived. He was smart enough to pack his damaged tunic so he could leave immediately. While it did not fit as nicely, his second tunic would be fine until he got his other repaired. He mounted his horse and rode off. The ride from town to her village was about the same hour it had been each time and once he got to the village he headed directly to her home. His nerves once again hit him as he dismounted. If she rejected him, it would probably be heartbreaking. The 'Open' sign was on the door so he took a deep breath and then opened the door. The first thing that hit him was the burning incense of the room. This time it smelled like some type of flower.

He heard Marah say before he turned around, "Welcome back Rone."

Turning around he responded, "Thank you."

Everything in the room was still the same. Marah had her hair loosely tied into a tail behind her head. She was wearing a bright pink dress with a bold white flower centered on her chest that spun off to the right with the green stem of the flower wrapping around the dress. It was a very unique looking dress that he had never seen anything like before.

"What brings you here?" She asked.

Raising his folded tunic up, he walked up to her and showed it to her before saying, "I was out on a scouting mission and a tree branch tore the lining off my right sleeve."

She grinned at him before stating, "I'm happy that you thought of me."

"No one else came to mind." He stated honestly.

Reaching out with her right hand she took the tunic from him. Her hand brushed against his own and he felt a little electricity in his mind. Her skin was quite soft. She examined the tunic closely and fiddled with the gold lining that was torn off.

"If you want to wait I can fix it right now."

He nodded at her before saying, "Okay."

Taking the same seat that he sat in last time, he watched as she set his tunic down before collecting some thread and a needle. He decided to wait until she finished before asking her if she wanted to go on the picnic with him. Reaching into his pocket, he pulled out the General's coin and fiddled with it below the counter. He was once again nervous but looking at her diligently working on his tunic let him know that he was on the right path.

As she started slowly sewing the golden lining into the sleeve she asked, "Anything else brought you here?"

He had wanted to wait until she finished her work but since she asked he decided to request her join him for a picnic.

He brought up the General's coin and set it on the counter before stating, "I spoke with your uncle, the General, earlier today and requested permission to court you and he said yes."

She suddenly flinched and then dropped her work while calling out, "Ouch!"

He guessed that she must have stabbed herself with the needle that she was working with since she brought her finger up to her mouth and sucked on it. He felt bad to have distracted her.

After a moment, with her finger still in her mouth, she asked, "He did?"

34

Deciding to be completely upfront with her he answered, "Yes. I was wondering if you would be interested in joining me for a picnic?"

Moving her finger away as a smile crossed her face as she replied, "I would be delighted to."

He grinned widely. Everything went according to plan and it was obvious that his mother was right, as usual.

"Are you free tomorrow at lunchtime?"

"Yes. I was hoping that you would ask." She stated.

He flushed lightly before commenting, "I would have asked sooner but I had to wait for the General to return from his visit in the Capital since I had missed him due to a mission."

"I'm just happy you asked." she joyfully said.

It was crystal clear that all his nervousness was for nothing. She was as attracted to him as he was to her.

Picking up her needle, she continued working and then asked, "Would you like me to pack lunch for the picnic?"

Answering her as he watched her work he said, "If you could, that would be wonderful. Being a military man, I'm used to eating whatever I can so pack whatever you prefer to eat."

"We'll have to correct that in the future. Could you bring a blanket, something to drink, and an umbrella?"

"An umbrella?" He asked.

"Yes. Something big. I've got sensitive skin that burns easily under the sun."

"Consider it done." He resolutely informed her.

She finished sewing the lining back into his tabard.

"How much do I owe you for the work?" He asked.

"Nothing. If you're going to be courting me, the least I could do is show you some of the benefits I would be able to provide as a wife."

"You're too kind Marah."

She passed the tunic over to him. This time it seemed as though she purposely caused their hands to make contact as she held the tunic and did not let go when their hands touched. He could get used to physical contact with her.

"Thank you. So, I'll see you tomorrow?" She asked.

"Tomorrow." He said with a nod.

She released his tunic. He stepped away and started to walk towards the door.

As he opened the door Marah called out, "Rone."

Turning to look at her he responded, "Yes?"

"If you shave your beard, it might increase the likelihood that you may receive a tender kiss on the cheek."

"Marah!" Henri called out.

Rone did not even notice that Henri was in the room.

Huffily she turned to Henri and responded, "What? I'm not saying he will receive a kiss; I'm just saying that the likelihood of that happening would greatly increase if he were clean shaven."

Rone immediately knew that he would be shaving his beard first thing tomorrow.

"There will be no kissing." Henri stated firmly.

Marah had a resolute look on her face before she stated, "I'll decide that on my own Henri and as I stated, the likelihood of a kiss happening will increase based on the state of his facial hair. We're officially courting now so I'll decide when and what happens, not you."

Getting an evil look on his face he turned to Henri and stated, "Consider me shaved."

Before an argument could ensue, he exited the building. He was certain that he saw Marah grin as he made his statement.

Chapter 6

Waking up early the next morning, Rone could do little but lay on his bed and grin widely. After the Leftenant returned with the men, Rone requested the day off so he could spend time with Marah. Her comment about showing her potential as a wife let him realize that courting her would most likely lead to marriage. It was not something he had thought about in his life, but now it was something that he looked forward to. Thoughts about having to purchase a home in town for them and of course stocking it with everything Marah would need hit him. He realized that all those years saving most of his pay was for a purpose that he did not even realize. Standing up, he got dressed. Since he was not working, he decided to first go to the bathing house and then collect everything Marah asked him to bring. Today he was going to wear a nice blue tunic and a pair of brown trousers. It was his favorite civilian clothing since it matched his eyes wonderfully. He made sure to shave his beard off and apply some lotion to his face to make his skin as soft as possible. After cleaning up, he ate a light breakfast and then went to the Requisitions Officer to ask for an umbrella. They were kind enough to issue him one. He strapped it onto the side of his saddle. He tucked a large blanket into his saddlebag and then bought a bottle of wine for them to drink while eating lunch. Since it was slightly over an hour and a half before he had to meet Marah, he headed off. He wanted to find a location in her village where they could sit together and eat.

Once he arrived in her village he stopped next to a middle-aged man and asked, "Sir is there a good spot near the village within walking distance that would make for a fine picnic location?"

The man, who was wearing a tan tunic, gray trousers, and a pair of normal sandals, answered, "If you go north of the village there is a wide field near a pond that is a popular location for people to swim and enjoy a nice meal."

"Thank you sir." Rone told the man sincerely.

"You're welcome."

Rone continued riding to Marah's home. Since it would not be appropriate for her to ride on his horse with him, they would have to walk. He saw no issue since it would allow them to spend more time together. He could think of nothing that he looked forward to more than this picnic with Marah. As he approached her house, he was surprised to see that she was already outside waiting for him with a basket in hand. She waved at him, which he responded to with a wave back. She was wearing a full length red dress that had long sleeves with golden material on the cuffs. The dress was belted by a gold colored sash and the bottom of the dress had the same golden colored material on the edges of it. He could see she had red open-toed sandals on her feet. Her hair was braided into one long braid and then circled into a bun on the back of her head. She looked simply wonderful.

As he rode up he said, "Good morning Marah."

"Good morning to you."

He dismounted his horse and tied it to the rack in front of her home. As he turned around Marah extended a hand towards him in greeting.

He took her hand softly and said, "I'm excited about spending the afternoon with you."

"As am I."

Gesturing with his other hand he said, "Let me get the umbrella and we'll head off."

"Okay."

He pulled out the bottle of wine and passed it to her. She took it and tucked it into her basket. He then took out the blanket and flipped it over his left shoulder before removing the umbrella and leaning it against his left shoulder on top of the blanket.

"Shall we?" he asked while holding out his free right hand.

She placed her hand on top of his right wrist with her fingers settling on the back of his hand and her thumb wrapped around his wrist before replying, "Lead on sir."

Looking at her he grinned before guiding her towards the north.

"Where are we headed?" She asked.

"There is a field near a pond north of here I am told has a lovely field."

"I know it well." She informed him.

He loved the feel of her hand holding onto his and knew immediately it was something he could grow used to.

As they walked, she stated, "You look so much younger clean shaven. Really barely much older than I am."

He chuckled at her before stating, "Why do you think I grew it out? I'm very young for my rank so I thought looking older might help my command appearance."

She giggled before stating, "I'd say looking handsome is more important than some command appearance."

He recognized a compliment when he heard one, so he told her, "Thank you. I think you're beautiful."

Shifting her weight, she nudged his arm with her shoulder before saying, "Thank you."

Her personality really was delightful.

"Can I confess something to you Rone?"

"Of course."

"I just turned seventeen and have known for some time that I did not wish to wait long until I was married."

"Okay…"

"Instead of letting my uncle Gerrard just randomly pick a future husband I let him know precisely the type of man that I wanted and found attractive."

Rone said nothing as she continued, "I don't know how he found you but if I were to picture exactly what I wanted my husband to look like in my mind, it was literally you."

"You're too kind."

"I hope that you're not offended by my uncle's mechanizations to arrange the match."

Giving a light chuckle he stated, "I'm not. I find myself quite pleased and if I'm honest with you, my mother had told me a few days ago that it was planned out. I'm not surprised my mother was right, she usually is."

Marah laughed loudly before stating, "I can't wait to meet her."

"Maybe on a future date?" He inquired.

"Possibly. We should see how this one goes before we commit to more."

She pointed off to a field on the left before stating, "It's over there."

"Alright." He responded while guiding her through the field.

He could see why it was a popular place. It had a few trees and was very flat. There were already three different groups of people there, two of which appeared to be families.

"Let's set up over there." Marah said while pointing to a spot near the pond but not so close that they could get wet.

He guided her to the spot and once they were there, she released her hold on his arm. He almost wished that he could have kept her hand there forever. Shifting the umbrella, which he set down, he pulled out his blanket and laid it out flat. He then picked up the umbrella and opened it. Glancing up to see where the sun was aiming down at them, he stabbed the umbrella into the ground so that it would obstruct the sun while they sat on the blanket. Marah set down the basket and then sat down next to it. He was unsure at first where to sit but decided he wished to sit directly next to her. He sat down and looked at her. She turned away from fiddling with the basket to look at him. She smiled, which he returned with a big grin.

"I've made us some flat bread with tomato sauce and covered it in cheese. I've also sliced some olives, some fresh berries, and a few pieces of cheese."

"It sounds delicious." He told her.

She passed him a large plate and then placed one piece of flat bread, a handful of olives, some berries, and a few pieces of cheese. Rone picked up the bottle of wine and used his knife to open it. Thankfully Marah was wise enough to include two glasses, so he poured some wine into each and then set one down in front of the both of them. Marah served herself a plateful of food and then picked up the glass of wine.

Rone picked up his own glass and then asked, "A toast?"

She inclined her head towards him as a sign of agreement. He then said, "To our future together."

As she leaned her cup towards his, he lightly tapped it.

"Here, here." She replied.

It took a sip. The wine was not a strong one, but it had a nice, sweet flavor that would accompany most meals. She drank a sip of her wine and smiled. He really liked her smile quite a bit.

"Rone I was wondering, if our courtship is a success and we're married, will we live in Durnovaria?"

"It would be ideal since an hour ride to town both ways would be unpleasant to do every day since I am stationed in Durnovaria."

"I'm excited about living in town as every time I've gone it has been wonderful. I had always assumed that people in the bigger town would be less pleasant than in my village but that has not been the case."

He chuckled at her before saying, "I agree. I've found most fellow citizens to be kind people."

She shifted her body so that she was sitting slightly closer to him. He took a moment to take a bite of the flat bread. The tomato sauce made it taste nice.

"How is it?"

"Very pleasant thank you."

"I made it all myself. Auntie has been teaching me all the skills a woman would need to be a proper wife."

"Compliments to both the cook and your aunt."

She reached out a hand and poked his side.

Raising an eyebrow at her he asked, "Yes?"

"Henri is spying on us."

Shrugging he stated, "Let him. I'm just happy to be here with you."

"Me too! The moment you first walked into my store I was stunned by how you were exactly what I had imagined my future husband would look like. How did my uncle find you?"

"I've got no idea. I've only met the General one time, so I didn't know him well at all."

"When did you meet him?"

"He presented me with the Golden Cross."

"What is that?"

"It's the highest military honor one can receive for valor in combat."

She shuffled and moved even closer. Now she was sitting so close to him that if she moved any closer, she would be pressed up against him. He could now smell whatever perfume she was wearing, and it was lovely.

He told her, "I can only imagine that he took whatever requirements you gave him and then had his officers find the man who fit the bill. I'm just pleased that I was his selection."

"I hope he wasn't too stern when you asked."

"He wasn't. I think he probably appreciated me standing up for my honor when he questioned me about my intentions."

She nodded before stating, "He told me when we spoke about what I was looking for in a man that no matter what I wanted, the man would have to be able to stand up to him and hold himself in high honor. I must confess however that I did lie to you earlier."

Glancing over at her he asked, "How so?"

"When I told you we were delivering cream buns to him, which we did do, our primary purpose was to discuss you. He said

42

the fact that not only you met my physical requirements but was his best enlisted soldier in the division meant you were his choice, even if I had decided I didn't find you attractive. He said something about him knowing more about men than I did. He was very pleased when I told him that I felt you were perfect for me. Henri mocked me for being clumsy around you."

"I found you quite charming and I'm starting to really like your uncle." Rone stated with a chuckle.

She giggled before saying, "He's a big softie. I bet he even threatened you if you broke my heart."

"He did. The Major suggested that your cousin Henri would attempt to rough me up if I hurt your feelings."

Leaning into him she whispered in his ear, "I guess you better not hurt my feelings then."

As she moved away from him, he stated, "I've got no intentions of doing so."

She then asked, "Do you fear that I might hurt your feelings?"

Turning to look at her, he thought that it would be unpleasant if she did so.

He answered, "No."

She grabbed him by the arm and stated, "Big strong man."

"I try." He told her.

"How many siblings do you have?"

"Three brothers and two sisters. I'm the oldest. And you?"

"As I said, I'm an orphan but I have two older cousins who have been like brothers to me. Duarde and Henri."

"I've met Henri, where is Duarde?" He asked.

"He's stationed in the Capital."

Military tended to be a family tradition. He hoped if he had sons that they would either pursue being officers or something outside of the military.

Marah interrupted his thoughts, "Rone."

"Yes?"

"I would like to see you again."

He grinned at her before saying, "Me too. I was thinking that I could rent a carriage and we could go see my mother."

"That would be lovely. Also… I wouldn't object if you felt a sudden urge to kiss me."

Rone leaned forward and kissed her. She responded to his kiss eagerly.

Chapter 7

Rone grunted when the Leftenant announced their new orders. They were ordered to travel to the village of Portsmouth, a coastal village, to deal with a possible sighting of goblins. Of all the beasts that they fought; he hated fighting goblins the most. Normal battle strategies would not work. He and his men would have to plow into the ranks of the goblins and fight them hand to hand after a volley or two of arrows. It was the only combat that he worried men could get seriously hurt. Goblins were just too nimble and numerous to fight in normal formation. Rone mounted his horse and fell in line with the formation. This mission was going to require more than his 50-man platoon, so they were assigned with two other platoons to be led under a senior officer. Their ride to Portsmouth was a half day and then they set up camp before the senior leadership met to plan what to do. Rone patiently waited and let the officers coordinate their plans and then issued it out to everyone. He reviewed their plan, which was to send out rapid scouting teams to find the goblins before sending the main force to engage. Thankfully the officers knew the strategies needed to fight goblins, so orders were issued to bring the right gear for the fight. He just wanted to make sure his men survived.

The Leftenant announced to the men, "We've got our orders and Sergeant Millar will break down the tasking for each of you. I understand fighting these beasts is particularly difficult, so I want to impress the importance of working together. Sergeant Millar…"

Rone stepped up and had the Non-Commissioned Officers approach and then issued the plan to each one. The plan called for scouting teams to head out immediately to ensure no goblins were nearby and then the next day a full survey would happen. He sent out the two scout teams and then set the rest of the men to set up camp for the time they would be there. While he had only been on one date with Marah he found he missed her already. Their kisses at the picnic were quite the experience. She was also a little more handsy than he expected. Originally the plan was to take her to meet his mother in two days but this mission came down, which could take up to a week or so, so he had to let her know that he would not be able to see her again until his return. He, of course, sincerely apologized to her and promised that he would make it up to her when he returned. The plan he came up with was to buy her flowers as a small token of affection and an apology for the delay.

The Leftenant's voice calling out broke Rone out of his thoughts, "Sergeant Millar are the men briefed?"

He turned to the Leftenant and responded, "Yes sir. Our scout team has already left and the men are setting up camp."

"Fine work. The Colonel has called another meeting. I'll return if anything of note is required to share."

"Yes sir."

Likely it was more of an Officer bonfire and social hour than a meeting. Rone was not new to the military and he knew that Officers tended to be of a higher social status and looked down on the troops from a social aspect. Really, it was quite surprising that the General was so willing for an enlisted man to court his niece. Maybe the General was not like the other Officers he dealt with or maybe he was that impressed with Rone. Whatever it was, he was quite happy. His mind was constantly shifting back to thoughts about her. He could not wait until he could introduce her to his mother. There was no doubt that his mother was be quite excited to have such a lovely and personable daughter-in-law. They must have kissed ten or so times sitting at that picnic before he took her back home. He suspected that Henri was not there to stop them from bonding through conversation and limited physical contact but to keep her safe. He did not blame her family at all in their efforts in keeping her safe. Soon, it would be his duty to protect her. If he someday had daughters he would act exactly as her family had. It was a man's duty to protect his wife, his children and any other women in his family. A proper honorable man would die to perform his duty and Rone was such a man.

Sergeant Clarke returned from his scouting trip and as he walked up to Rone he said, "Sergeant, we've returned from our initial scouting trip and there was no enemy spotted."

"Very good Sergeant Clarke. Go settle your men down and get some supper. Tomorrow morning at first light we'll be sending both Scout teams out."

"Yes Sergeant."

With his men settled down for the night Rone decided that it was time to lie down on his bedding, which was nothing more than a fur mat and a blanket that he would use to cover himself. He closed his eyes and drifted off to sleep thinking about Marah.

* * * * *

Someone nudged Rone to wake him. He opened his eyes to see that it was the Leftenant.

"Sergeant, it's time to get ready. The scouts must head out so we can find where the goblins are at and then send our bulk forces to deal with them."

"Yes sir." Rone said as he stood up.

After taking a moment to get ready, he issued orders to send both of the scout teams out. He suspected that they would find the enemy pretty quickly. The rumor was that these goblins were heading from the east to Portsmouth. The encampment was set up right outside the eastern border of the village. Rone took some time to eat a simple breakfast from his personal stores that he kept in his saddlebags. He heard rumors that the Colonel had argued for a cavalry charge against the goblins. Rone knew one time this was tried it was disastrous for the poor horses. The goblins were so quick with their daggers that they seriously hurt a whole platoon's horses. Thankfully several other officers had heard about the one platoon so that idea was scrapped. Rone took time to inspect the soldiers from his platoon who were still waiting. They were all decked out in plated armor that covered their legs, front and back, and a breastplate. He had them wear a helmet with a plated gorget. It would allow them to serve almost as an armored beast against the swarming goblins. This was probably going to be ugly but sometimes fighting was not pretty. No shields would be used in this fight since they would slow down the men. Word came out and the orders were soon issued. The goblins were spotted several leagues to the east.

Rone yelled out, "Form up!"

His soldiers responded by forming a marching formation. He fell into line and waited for orders from the Colonel, an older man with peppered and trimmed gray hair. He was clean shaven with sharp blue eyes. He was wearing the same battle uniform the rest of the men wore. Rone knew that he would never see combat but was always playing the part.

The Colonel yelled out, "Sergeant Major, take charge of the formation and let's go deal with these monsters!"

"Yes sir!" The Sergeant Major said.

The Sergeant Major was the most senior Non-Commissioned Officer in Durnovaria. He was wearing the same battle armor. His short shock-white hair was neatly trimmed with a cleanly shaven face. His eyes were dark brown. He took his place in front of the formation and saluted the Colonel.

As the Colonel returned the salute and walked away, the Sergeant Major called out, "Move out!"

Each formation began marching. Rone reflected on the battle plan. Each platoon would split, with his platoon serving as the right flank as the cap of the whole formation. His platoon was chosen because of their experience in battle. As they finally got to the positions the platoons spread out. Rone guided his men into position and set them up in a double line formation. He had his best fighters in the first rows, especially the ones with the most time fighting goblins. Rone himself was normally supposed to stand behind the ranks but that was not how he fought. He instead stood in the middle of the front row. The Leftenant wanted to stand next to him but Rone convinced the man it was his job to manage the lines from behind the formation. The sun was finally up and it was not long until Rone could see the goblins starting to come into view. For some reason the number of goblins seemed unusually high. It took him a moment to realize that the goblins must have seen them move into battle positions and then decided to try and sweep right and around them.

Turning back to the Leftenant Rone yelled out, "Sir. We must send a runner to the Colonel to let him know the goblins have shifted and are all coming at our platoon."

"I understand Sergeant."

Rone heard the Leftenant telling one of the many Privates within the platoon what he needed to know. It was then that Rone realized they would need to shift their formation slightly to the right in order to force the goblins to come within charging range.

He bellowed out, "Shift 15 degrees to the right. Wait on my orders to charge."

The men moved to the right and maintained their formation. He was still marked in the center of the formation. The goblins were now about half of a league away.

"Ready your swords!" Rone yelled as he drew his gladius.

Rone knew immediately from the numbers of goblins that many of his men were about to be injured or even killed. They needed to stall the creatures long enough for the others to arrive.

As the goblins were a mere 7 or 8 paces away Rone yelled out, "Charge!"

Giving out a loud bellow he raced forward. He knew that the men would follow him and he was not disappointed. Swinging downward, Rone slashed his sword into the head of the first goblin he met. Next, he used his foot to violently boot the body of the next one. The creatures were fragile and its ribs fractured from the force of Rone's blow. He felt the crude daggers slashing and bouncing off his armor. He was quite thankful for the armor to protect them. Swinging like a farmer chopping down wheat, a useful skill he learned from his father as a child, he cleaved through the goblins. Rone glanced around to his left and right. His men were holding their own but he spotted that some men had fallen. It was not going as well as he would have liked.

Gesturing back, Rone called out, "Fill my rank!"

One of his men stepped in. Rone dashed over to his right and helped the men in trouble with goblins. He lashed out with his sword and struck down a goblin before using his other hand to reach out and slap down another goblin. He spun about with his sword and sliced at two goblins who had knocked the man down. Pushing forward, he slapped the side of his sword to stun one goblin while continuing the blow forward into the chest of another.

Rone called out, "Circle up!"

He grabbed one of his injured men with his free arm and slashed out with his sword while pulling backwards to bring the injured man with him. The men around him formed into that circle as well. He continued slashing his sword forward. A trio of goblins charged directly at him. He brought his sword forward and lashed out to strike the first one before trying to continue the swing into the next one. The other two moved so quickly that they got past his sword and barreled right into him. He had miscalculated the swing enough that he was put off balance. The force of the two goblins landing on him caused him to fall backwards with the goblins on top of him. He brought his free arm up and slammed it into the first goblin. The second one slashed his arm and cut deeply into his forearm with it. Rone grimaced in pain but fought on by reaching out with his injured arm and grabbing the goblin by the throat to squeeze its neck. He used his sword-arm and stabbed the goblin in the chest. Its blood splattered all over Rone's face and chest. While pulling the sword out, he squeezed as hard as he could, which due to the much smaller size of the goblin caused its neck to snap. The two goblins fell dead on top of him. Someone's hand reached out and helped Rone stand. As he got up, he saw that it was the Leftenant. They were struggling to hold their ground. A blaring echo of a war horn in the distance let Rone know that their reinforcements were there. His men cheered and began to fight with fervor. He joined them and pressed against the goblins. It must have been the sound of reinforcements that scared the goblins because they turned and started to run away.

The Leftenant bellowed out, "Press them men!"

Rone grinned at the orders of the Leftenant. The man learned quickly. Rone followed shoulder to shoulder with the others as they began to run down the goblins. Sadly, most were too fast and still managed to escape.

"Stop!" Rone called out since he knew that they could not catch the goblins.

They had won the day.

Chapter 8

Rone strolled out of the medical tent. He frowned heavily at the losses his platoon took. Over twenty men died, and every other man was injured. However, the reports he got from the field showed that the battle was an overall success. The goblins retreated to the mountain range and the count shown that exactly two hundred and thirty-three goblins were killed in battle. The Colonel roundly cheered the platoon, but it would be some time before the injured men would heal and the dead could be replaced. Rone spoke with the Leftenant and they now had to plan how to deliver the bad news to each man's family. It was the Officer's duty with his Non-Commissioned Officer to aid him. It was a task Rone had done many times but dreaded deeply each time. The only good news is the fact he was ordered back to Durnovaria. This meant that he would be able to have more time courting Marah. Glancing down at his heavily bandaged forearm he grunted. While the injury would help with breaking the news to his men's families, Marah was likely going to be very upset.

Walking up to the Leftenant, Rone said, "Sir, I'm going to head back with the men to Durnovaria as ordered. Will you be joining us or does the Colonel need you for other taskings?"

"Thank you Sergeant. The Colonel has asked me to assist his staff in planning the clean-up missions to give me more field experience. I'll return to town in a week."

"Yes sir. If it is okay with you sir, I'll release the men for leave while you are away."

"That works Sergeant. I'll see you in a week."

"Yes sir." Rone told him before walking away.

As he mounted his horse, he gestured to the injured who could ride and the uninjured men to mount up. They followed his lead as they slowly rode off. They would return to Durnovaria early tomorrow and Rone would send word to Marah immediately to see her the next day. Hopefully she was available.

* * * * *

Rone woke up the next day. His arm was in quite a bit of pain from the deep cut that foul goblin gave him. The medics had provided him with ointments to deal with the cut and keep it from getting infected but there was nothing that they could do outside of some minor pain numbing ointments. Since the cut was bandaged and they told him not to remove it because they would do so in a few days for his check up, he was forced to suffer through the pain. The best news, he was able to rent a small carriage that would fit two and had a cover to protect Marah from the sun. It came with one large horse and a repair kit, just in case. He was excited about introducing Marah to his mother. He cleaned up, which was made difficult by having to avoid getting his bandage wet, and then got a light breakfast. It was not long before he was on the road with the carriage. His only concern would be Marah's reaction to his injury. Sure, she knew that he was in the military, but Rone suspected she would not have realized the dangers of his career until she saw him today. It really was a great idea he rented this carriage from the elderly man back in town, the sun was out, and it was quite bright. It made for a lovely ride. He rode the carriage through her village after a pleasant ride that was slightly over an hour. As he turned down the path towards Marah's home, he spotted her standing outside her home waiting for him. She was wearing a simple tan dress with a wide brown leather belt. She was holding an umbrella over her head. Her hair was styled into two braids that started on the back of her head and dropped behind her. She waved excitedly at him when she spotted him in the carriage. He waved back at her. Standing next to her was her cousin Henri.

As his carriage pulled up Marah said, "Hello Rone!"

Grinning at her, he stopped the carriage and then said, "Good afternoon."

Rone climbed out of the carriage and as he turned to face her, she frowned. He realized immediately that she must have finally seen the bandage on his arm.

She jogged up to him and took his injured arm with her hands before asking in a very concerned sounding voice, "What happened to your arm?"

He did not want her to panic about the seriousness of his injury, so he stated, "It's just a scrape."

It was obvious that she did not believe him because she stated, "They don't bandaged scrapes so strongly. I know you're a big strong man but don't sugar coat it to me mister."

She clearly had a little more sass to her and was a more intelligent than she had let on, so he just answered honestly, "A trio of goblins knocked me down in battle and while I stabbed two, one got me in the forearm with its dagger."

Cradling his arm closer she said, "I'm sorry you got hurt Rone. Is there anything I can do to help you feel better?"

"Marah." Henri grumpily said.

"Not like that Henri! I'm just worried for my future husband's safety."

"I'll be fine. Shall we go? My mother is very excited to meet you today." He stated.

"Okay." She told him.

He lifted his arm once again for her to take. Once she set her hand on his, he guided her to the other side of the carriage and helped her enter. After she was seated, he strolled around and climbed in.

"Henri." He said while turning to look at her cousin.

"Yes?"

"Don't worry, I'll keep her safe."

"I know." Henri stated before walking away.

Rone tapped the reins to start the carriage off. Marah shifted a little closer to him and wrapped her arms around his right arm. He grinned as she tenderly ran her fingers over his hand and then placed his hand on her lap over her dress. They were a little handsy in the park but nothing like this and he was greatly enjoying it.

Once they left the village she asked, "Maybe I should ask my father to promote you to a safer job, so I don't have to fear for your safety?"

Rone frowned. He loved what he was doing, and he did hear rumors that there was talk about promoting him, but he wanted to earn his promotion, not have it handed to him because he was courting the General's niece.

"Please don't do that. I'd like to earn my promotions through merit not relationships."

She grinned at him before stating, "I already tried, and my uncle told me no. He said you would be insulted to be promoted without earning it."

"I really like your uncle. A man who gains something unearned doesn't value it like a man who sweats for it."

"You're just too sexy… I swear its taking everything I have to keep from melting all over you like a spoon of butter on a baked potato."

Rone chuckled before saying, "I'm thinking our courting might be a short one, I'd very much like you to melt all over me."

Marah laughed uproariously at him. He laughed with her. There was indeed quite a bit of sexual tension between them that only seemed to grow during their picnic between each kiss. Marah suddenly looked back behind them. He was unsure what she was looking for.

"I was worried we were being followed." She stated.

Shrugging at her he commented, "There is no reason to follow us. I'm courting you and really at this point, we're going to be married. Your family likely have accepted it."

"Well," Marah said before taking a slight pause and then continuing, "Since we're going to eventually get married, I might as well take advantage of the benefits."

She let go of his arm and then slid sideways onto his lap. He could smell her wonderful perfume since she was now sitting on his lap with her arms wrapped around his neck.

"I hope you don't mind." She stated while looking at him.

Rone chuckled, she seemed to be a bit more aggressive than he had initially thought that she would be. He greatly liked it and once they finally married, he suspected they would have a lot of fun together in bed.

"I'll take that as a no."

"Of course. I spend most of my free time thinking of you."

She gave him a deeply passionate kiss. Rone thought to himself, yes, it was going to be a short courtship.

"Me too." Marah said to him after she stopped kissing him.

She slipped her right arm off him and then rested her head on his shoulder. They sat there quietly enjoying their ride together. It was another hour before they got to Peel. Marah slid off his lap when the town came into view. It was important that they maintained dignity around others, so he understood. Once they got to the farmhouse his mother lived in, he stopped the carriage and then helped Marah exit. She took his arm once again and he guided her to the door.

As he opened the door he called out, "Mother I'm home with a guest."

The moment he started to speak he heard his youngest brother Mavin running right away. It was a matter of a second before Mavin came into view. Rone released Marah and caught Mavin as he crashed into him.

Mavin asked immediately, "Who's this?"

"This is the girl I told you about."

"Ewww. I guess you lost then."

Rone laughed heartily before saying, "Afraid so."

Mavin hugged him and then jumped off and started to run.

"Lost?" Marah asked.

56

Turning to her he chuckled before answering, "A joke. The last time I visited he asked if I was fighting orcs and I told him I was fighting a girl. He's young so it was just an easier way to explain things."

She took his arm again as she said, "I'll take the victory then."

He chuckled at her, and she winked at him. He heard his mother approaching.

"Rone... She's as lovely as you said she was."

Marah released her hold on him and then took his mother's hands as she said, "Thank you kindly ma'am."

"It's a pleasure to meet you, Marah, right?" His mother said.

"Yes ma'am."

Gesturing to the chairs in her main living area, his mother said, "Please come take a seat."

Rone guided her to a seat and sat down next to her. She continued to hold his hand as they sat next to each other.

His mother looked puzzled for a moment before asking, "Rone dear, what happened to your arm."

"War wound." He stated evenly.

His mother looked thoughtful for a moment before shifting to Marah and saying, "Tell me all about you."

Marah grinned, "I was adopted as a 6-year-old orphan by my uncle and aunt. My uncle is the commanding general of the regional military forces. My auntie runs a seamstress store that she opened recently. I work there for my auntie while learning everything she said I need to know to be a good wife. I have two cousins, Duarde and Henri. I make my own clothing and I'm very excited about being with your son."

"And he wants his niece to marry an enlisted man?" His mother asked.

Rone had to admit it was a reasonable question to ask because most officers tended to be from the upper class of citizenry in the kingdom. The enlisted men, like Rone, were from the lower classes. After all, his family were farmers.

Marah answered, "He told me that my husband had to be an honorable man who would treat me with dignity and respect. I told him the physical features I preferred and my uncle said that Rone was the best choice in the whole region. I personally don't care about silly stuff like high or low class. I just wanted a husband who would be kind and caring. Also, really good looking helped."

His mother chuckled and then stated, "He's a good boy."

Marah giggled before saying, "He's also so handsome. I was ready to marry him the moment he walked into my aunt's shop."

Rone chuckled. She was staring at him intently when he first met her, something he was equally guilty of.

His mother stood up and asked, "Will you be staying for supper?"

Nodding at her Rone answered, "We will but right afterwards I have to get her home."

Chapter 9

A week after taking Marah to see his mother, Rone found out the wine festival was returning to town so he decided to ask Marah if she wanted to go with him. She said that she was very happy about going since the last two times she was old enough to go when the annual wine festival would come to town, her family was busy. He had to rent another carriage for them since she was a lady and it was not appropriate for her to ride a horse. The plan would be to pick her up from her home, bring her to the festival, and then leave her for the night to stay at the General's residence in town. She told him that she was going to spend a few days with her uncle before being escorted back home. He wanted to take her home, but his platoon finally had enough men that they were going to be sent out on a mission tomorrow. Rone really felt horribly about not taking care of Marah like he wanted to but she insisted on finally going to the festival so he had to work with what he had so he could see her pleased, which was something he wanted to do.

Strolling up to the Leftenant Rone asked, "Sir, will we be giving the men the day off for the festival?"

"Yes Sergeant. I'll be attending, will you?"

"Yes sir."

"See you there Sergeant." The Leftenant said before he walked off.

Rone grinned. He loved giving the men time off for events, especially things like the festival. As he walked back to the barracks he reflected on what the men would think about Marah. He usually did not share his personal life with the men so they were likely going to be quite surprised by the fact he was courting the General's niece.

As soon as he entered the barrack he heard someone call out, "At ease!"

"Form up men!" Rone called out.

The men ran to their positions by their bunks. He loved how efficient they were. Rone strode up to his usual position where he would stand when announcing anything to them.

"Men. The Leftenant has decided that we're off today for the festival."

They cheered loudly. He grinned. Last year they missed the festival because they had to shift out to a small village a few dozen leagues away to deal with a bandit gang that was harassing citizens. Rone and his men crushed them mercilessly.

"Report time tomorrow is at sunrise. Have fun." Rone called out before he spun on his heel and walked away from them.

He walked along enjoying the day. It was another lovely day, spring really was the best time of year in his mind. The same old man that he rented a carriage from loaned him the same carriage. He paid the man and then headed off. Rone spent almost every day in the last few days thanking the gods. Rone just felt like everything was going his way lately, even with the goblin stabbing his forearm. Today he was planning to ask Marah if he should go ahead and ask her uncle for permission to marry her. He also started looking for a home for them. It was not as easy as he had hoped it would be. The market was complex and he was not exactly a wealthy man. He was planning to show her the three possible options before the festival started. The hooves of the horse pulling the carriage clopped along loudly and was the only sound he could hear. It was almost relaxing to hear as the horse steadily pulled the carriage. As he turned the carriage down the roadway towards Marah's home, he spotted her standing outside with Henri again. She looked beautiful as usual. Her hair was braided into a long braid and then spun into a bun along the back of her head. She was wearing a flowing long dress that was a light green color that had white ruffling along the hems of her sleeves and the bottom of the dress. Around her waist was a white belt that matched the ruffles. She was holding a white umbrella.

Once he pulled up to her home she said, "Hello Rone. It's pleasant to see you again."

Pulling his reigns to stop the carriage he stated, "My day grows better every time that I see you."

Marah smiled happily at his kind words. As he climbed off the carriage, she took his hand.

"Thank you." She told him.

After helping her sit in the carriage Rone climbed in himself and they headed off. Marah slide on the carriage seat until she was sitting closely next to him. He reached over with his free hand and placed it on her left thigh. She took a hold of his hand resting on her leg.

Marah announced, "I'm quite excited about the festival."

"No doubt. I went to the one the year before last and it was quite a bit of fun. Most people from the surrounding villages come to town just for it. It's a great way to honor the gods and celebrate the season."

Wanting to get a kiss, he leaned into her and kissed her on the lips. She responded to his kiss passionately. After kissing for a moment he leaned back to look forward.

Neither spoke for a while before Rone broke the silence, "I see no reason for us to keep waiting so I was wondering if you would be fine with asking your uncle for permission to marry you."

She squeezed his hands tightly before responding, "I would like that. I'm ready to start my own family and I feel as though we're a perfect match."

He grinned. He felt she was perfect for him as well. She was pleasant to be around, tender to him and his concerns, and she was very pleasing on the eyes.

"I'm glad to hear that. Before we go to the festival I thought we could examine the three possible homes I found within my budget."

"That sounds fun. I'm not too particular as long as it's safe and big enough for both us and a few children."

"Those were my requirements as well. I hope you find at least of them to your liking."

"I trust your judgment Rone. I'll gladly give input, but you know best."

He nodded. It was reassuring to be trusted so implicitly. There were more than a few occasional nights where he was concerned about his forthcoming responsibilities. He was about to become the sole provider for a woman and very likely several children in the near future. It was probably a wise choice to finally let the military leadership promote him to a First Sergeant position. The pay increase was significant and not purposely throwing himself into dangerous situations that could leave his family without a provider. He softly ran his fingers around and through her fingers that were holding his hand. He found her soft skin intoxicating. After a pleasant ride, they arrived in town and Rone guided the carriage to the first home that he found. He walked her through each of the homes and she clearly had a favorite of them, the largest and most expensive one. He figured it would last them for some time so he would communicate with the seller first thing tomorrow about arranging the purchase of it. He helped her enter their carriage and then they headed off to the festival. Usually it was held in a huge field to the east of the town, not in the town itself. Many troops were sent to the field to build the stands and help vendors set up shops. As he parked the carriage outside the field, he took a glance over at Marah. She had a look of wonderment when the festival came into sight. On the main stage was a musical ensemble that blared joyful music. In front of the stand was a huge crowd of people dancing. This festival was the happiest event of the year and plenty of wine would be drunk during the day.

"It's beautiful." Marah stuttered out, still with the look of awe on her face.

Rone chuckled. He had been to the festival several times so it was nothing new but he had to admit, the first time he saw it, he was in awe of it too.

"It is. Let's go in. There are plenty of stands with merchants and people who offer gifts." He stated.

Marah took his hand, and he began walking. It was quite exciting to bring her to the festival, not only because it was her first time going, but also because this was the first event that they were publicly announcing their relationship to the world. Before all of their dates were private affairs far from town and mostly people that Rone knew. The people at the festival seemed to be having fun and it immediately caused him to break out smiling. Glancing at Marah he saw her taking in the whole event. Her facial expression was a mixture of wonder and joy. He chuckled. It was a great pleasure to be able to be the first to show her something. Her hand holding his wrist was clinched tightly onto him. He spotted several of his men as they walked along but they did not approach him, which was normal when not attending military functions. Marah made him stop at one of the booths to purchase a sweet bread. She broke off a piece to feed him. Rone really loved her tenderness. As they walked back towards the main platform Rone noticed a long platform next to it that held the city leaders. He spotted Marah's uncle, the General, with what he assumed was her aunt and Henri, all sitting at a table.

As Rone observed the crowd he heard the familiar voice of the Leftenant, "Sergeant, it's a pleasure to see you here."

Rone looked at the man and gave him a smile. The Leftenant was with a woman who looked to be about Rone's age. She had dark brown hair that was pinned up into a bun on the back of her head, light brown eyes, and softly tanned skin. She was wearing a form-fitting blue dress with a white belt.

"You as well sir." Rone told him.

The Leftenant gestured to the woman before saying, "This is my wife Jessina."

Rone smiled at her before saying, "A pleasure to meet you Jessina. This is my fiancée Marah."

He turned towards Marah and gestured at her. Marah smiled.

The woman named Jessina was the first to speak, "Sergeant, Mattius has spoken very highly of you. It's a pleasure to meet you."

Grinning at her, Rone replied, "Thank you. It's an honor serving with your husband."

The Leftenant then said, "Marah, I swear you look familiar. Have I seen you somewhere before?"

Marah looked very confused for a moment before answering, "I don't think so, I rarely leave my uncle's home."

Suddenly the man who served as the assistant to the General, a Major approached and then asked, "Marah would you like to join your uncle?"

He gestured at the General.

Marah answered, "I'll appreciate the offer. Please tell my uncle that I belong with my future husband and he belongs here with his men."

The Major nodded before turning and then leaving.

There was a moment of silence before the Leftenant then said, "Oh! That's where I saw you before. I was part of a group reporting to the General when his family came to visit him a while ago."

Marah softly told him, "I apologize for not recognizing you. My uncle gets so many visitors that I have a hard time remembering them all."

"No problem at all Marah," The Leftenant replied before turning to Rone and continuing, "I'm curious how you ended up courting the General's niece."

Rone was unsure how to answer him. He really did not want to let the man know that it was mostly arranged.

Marah then announced, "My uncle picked the best man in his entire forces and arranged for us to meet. We felt a natural connection to each other and began our relationship immediately."

The Leftenant nodded thoughtfully. Rone did feel concern that others might see his relationship with Marah as him looking for an opportunity to advance his career. It was not the case since he legitimately held feelings for her.

Marah suddenly asked, "Could we go dance some?"

Rone flushed. He had to admit that he did not really know how to dance. It was not a skill needed to be a military man nor a farmer so he never learned.

Leaning over, he whispered in her ear, "I don't know how."

She turned to whisper back, "I'll teach you if you want."

He looked into her eyes, which she responded to by smiling at him.

Returning her smile, he said, "Okay."

Chapter 10

Rone strolled out of his quarters happily the next morning and headed off to the barracks to check up on his soldiers. As he walked up he saw the Leftenant waiting for him.

The Leftenant saluted him and then announced, "The Colonel asked me to send you to his office the moment you arrived."

Nodding at him, Rone said, "Yes sir.

He was wondering what the Colonel wanted but he immediately thought back to the last time he spoke with the man. The Colonel had offered him a promotion to First Sergeant. Rone had declined at the time and the Colonel did warn him the opportunities would be limited. Maybe the opportunity was about to present itself again. Shrugging off the thoughts he confidently walked to the division offices where the Colonel's office was. The offices were in a large building that had multiple rooms for each senior officer. It was a shared building for the entire division. Rone knocked loudly on the door of the Colonel's office.

A voice on the other side of the door said, "Enter."

Rone opened the door and stepped into the office. Like all officer offices at this level, there was a nice wood desk, a chair in front of it for a guest, a much nicer padded chair that the Colonel was sitting in, some shelves and a solid large book case. The Colonel skipped placing books on his book case and instead decorated it with several statures of horses. He clearly was a man who appreciated the animal. The Colonel himself was an older man, possibly only a few years younger than the General, with neatly trimmed peppered gray hair and a thin mustache of the same color. His skin was slightly pock-marked, likely from acne in his youth. His eyes were a light green color.

Standing in front of the Colonel's desk Rone said firmly, "Sir, Staff Sergeant Rone Millar reporting as ordered."

Rone gave the man a salute.

"Have a seat Sergeant Millar."

Glancing backwards slightly, Rone took a seat. The Colonel was usually a jovial man but he had a serious look on his face.

"Sergeant Millar it has come to my attention that you are about to take a bride. Is this true?"

Rone answered, "Yes sir."

The Colonel scratched his chin and looked thoughtful for a moment before saying, "This means its finally time for you to move up in your career."

Rone did not say a word. He was thinking the same thing, although he had to admit he would greatly miss serving with his men.

"I've already offered you the opportunity to serve as a First Sergeant but that position at the company level has already been filled."

Rone wondered what the man was looking for since there was not a lot of First Sergeant positions.

The Colonel continued speaking, "Luckily for you, the General himself has ordered the creation of a Battle Staff to begin to push the fight from our borders and out into the mountainside with the intent of pushing the monsters constantly threatening us away from town. Because of this, there is a new First Sergeant position that has been made within that Battle Staff. Due to your experience and skill in dealing with these monsters, I've personally suggested to the General that you would be the ideal man to fill that position. Before you answer I want to let you know that this might likely be your last opportunity to move into a First Sergeant position. A position that, I note, comes with a significant pay increase."

Rone was pleasantly surprised. One of his biggest concerns with the First Sergeant position was a lack of direct influence in battling the monsters that they faced regularly. He was still not done dishing out revenge to the creatures who hurt his family. This new post sounded interesting and would not only give him more pay but make Marah happier knowing that he would not be in the line of fire every day.

He decided to accept the officer so he said, "Sir. I want to thank you for the kind offer and let you know that I accept the new posting."

The Colonel rubbed his hands together before saying, "Excellent. We have many men deserving of promotion and when one stagnates in a post, it slows down everyone. I'll give you the day off to manage any personal business with your men and family. The tomorrow you're to report here to my office so I can introduce you to Captain Bainbridge, your new Officer in Charge."

"Yes sir, thank you."

"Dismissed." The Colonel announced.

Rone stood up and saluted the man before spinning on his heel and heading out. The first thought to cross his mind was the realization that he now had an excuse to visit Marah. He just got promoted so he would need his new rank stripe sewn into his tunic. It caused him to grin widely. Rone first went to the Leftenant's office to let him know the news and then he went to the barracks to let his men know. He was quite touched by the response of his men, they seemed legitimately upset he was leaving but happy for his promotion. After spending some time with the men, he wished them luck and then headed off. First, he went to his quarters to pick up his second tunic and then mounted his horse. It was an hour ride to Marah's home and it was a little rainy outside but that did not damper his mood. Once he finished with her, he would have to go back to the man selling the home that Marah preferred so he could begin the process of buying it. His hope was to ask for permission to marry her and then maybe a month later they would be able to wed and move into this home.

During the festival she had mentioned that her family offered to help with items for the home such as furniture. He saw no issues accepting help from her family to help them get settled. Rone dismounted his horse and tied the reins down before pulling out his second tunic out of the saddlebag. The 'Open' sign was on the door so he opened the doors and stepped in.

Marah's voice said, "Hello, how may I help you?"

She must not have been looking right away. She looked up right as he turned to face her.

"Rone!" She called out and she quickly walked up to him and gave him a hug.

He hugged her back tightly. He was unsure what perfume she was wearing but it smelled lovely.

As he let her go she asked, "What brings you here?"

"I've got great news."

"Oh really?"

Grinning at her he answered, "Yes. I've been promoted to First Sergeant for a special Battle Staff."

Clapping her hands Marah declared, "That's wonderful news! Congratulations Rone, you deserve it."

He glanced around to notice Henri was not in the room so he gave her a kiss, which she responded to by kissing him back energetically.

After he broke their kiss he asked, "Could you kindly add a rank stripe to my tunics for me?"

She took the tunics out of his hands as she said, "Of course!"

He sat down in the same stool that he had sat in before. Marah placed his tunic on her counter and then collected several items to get to work. He really liked to watch her as she stood there working on whatever it was she was doing. The look of concentration on her face was cute, especially when she would stick out her tongue a little bit when focusing intently.

As she worked, she asked, "Are you free tomorrow night?"

"I have my first day of working at my new post but afterwards I should be available."

"Auntie asked me to invite you to supper tomorrow night since my uncle will be home."

He chuckled. The family was pushing her right into his arms eagerly. He had to admit that she was not the first woman who a family tried to marry off to him. The neighbor of his brother had asked if he would be interested in their daughter. That was two years ago and at the time Rone was not interested in being married. He was thankful that he was not ready because Marah was significantly more attractive to him, especially with her unique appearance. Her light freckled skin and bright orange hair was very pretty. It was a subject that he felt not to mention since it might only just offend her more than serve any other purpose.

Rone told her, "I'll be there. It'll be the perfect opportunity to ask your father for your hand in marriage."

"That's what Auntie said. She also wants to meet you."

"I'm excited to meet her too." Rone stated.

Marah nodded as she continued working. He sat there quietly while she worked. After she finished both tunics, she passed them to him. She walked around the counter. He was still sitting in the chair.

Wrapping her arms around his shoulders she said, "I hope that you aren't upset Rone but I'm happy to hear that you'll be taken out of harm's way. I don't want to be without you."

"I understand. I'm pleased with this new post as it will allow me the chance to continue striking the monsters who killed my father while helping further my career and family."

Marah whispered in his ear, "I can't wait until we're married. I daydream about being in your arms every night."

He chuckled at her before whispering back, "I feel the same way. It's going to be a long month but I don't worry because then we'll have a lifetime together. Is it wrong to feel so strongly about someone you just met?"

70

"No. I barely know you and am already in love with you." Marah replied in a sultry tone.

He was finding it hard to resist taking her right there on the floor of her shop but he knew that he had to protect her dignity, not take it.

"I love you too, even though it seems so fast." He told her.

She pushed herself even closer into him. The warmth of her body threatened to overwhelm him, especially with the soft smelling perfume that she was wearing and whatever soaps she used on her hair.

Deciding it was best to step away in order to keep their dignity until marriage he stood up and announced, "I wish that I could make love to you but I must go and start the purchase of our home before someone else takes it."

Marah took a deep breath and smoothed out her dress before saying, "A wise idea."

He grinned at her, which she replied back by giving him a smile.

Giving her a tender kiss, he told her, "I'll see you tomorrow."

"I look forward to it." She replied.

Rone waved lightly and then strolled out of her home. He grabbed the reins of his horse and then mounted. The right back to town was the usual hour or so in a light rain. He enjoyed the rain quite a bit but an hour riding in it got tiresome. It did not deflect his overall happy mood however. His first stop was to the owner of the home that he was going to purchase for them. The man had not sold it yet so Rone immediately proposed to purchase it right there. Once the man agreed to a price, Rone went with the man to the bank. There they put in a transfer of funds and then the deed to the home was given to Rone. After they finished that, Rone had to submit the new deed to the town's tax services. One of the few advantages of being in the military was exempt from taxation but he still had to report the sale so the man selling it to him could be taxed and his rightful ownership is tracked.

Rone was very excited so he went back to his new home and immediately changed the locks on the doors to protect his new property. Sadly, he had nothing to put into the home so he headed back to his quarters.

Chapter 11

Rone woke up the next morning excited for his future. This new position was something very new and he imagined he would be the man to set the standard for the position and its future. After visiting the bath house and eating breakfast he confidently walked to the division offices. He looked forward to meeting his new Officer in Charge, a Captain Bainbridge. Rone saluted the various soldiers that saluted him as he walked. As he entered the division offices, he quickly moved to the office of the Colonel. He knocked loudly on the door.

"Enter."

Rone opened the door and stepped in. The office was exactly the same as yesterday and the Colonel looked the same. The only change was the second man standing in the office. He guessed that the man was Captain Bainbridge. He was tall, about the same height as Rone, and Rone guessed the man was in his early thirties. With short blonde hair and light blue eyes, the man had a clean-shaven face. He was wearing the traditional wine-red tunic, black trousers, and a pair of sandals.

Rone strolled up to the Colonel's desk and stopped before announcing as he saluted, "Sir. First Sergeant Rone Millar reporting as ordered."

He tried not to but he could not help but grin as he said his new rank. The Colonel returned the salute while sitting in his seat.

"Good morning First Sergeant. Let's just get right to business. This is Captain Bainbridge."

The Colonel gestured towards the man that Rone guessed was the Captain.

Before Rone could respond the Captain said, "Good morning First Sergeant Millar. I'm very excited to be working with you."

"Thank you sir, I'm excited about this unique opportunity as well."

The Captain turned to the Colonel and asked, "Sir may we be excused?"

The Colonel nodded at them.

"Follow me." The Captain ordered.

"Yes sir." Rone responded as he followed the Captain out of the office and then silently walked out of the division offices.

The Captain led Rone towards the South Gate as he spoke, "Our command center is going to be located in a specially designed fortification along the south wall that gives us an excellent view of the mountainside."

Rone said nothing as the man continued talking, "Our mission is to coordinate the defensive measures against our enemies within this mountain range and then plan special missions to work towards eliminating the desire of the enemy to continue attacking us."

"So not eradication?" Rone ask.

"No. Killing women, children, and elderly is not honorable. We just need to push their forces over to the other side of the mountain so that they will not continue attacking us. The primary goal there is to eventually set up a fortification near the main pass in the mountain range so that we can move the fight away from Durnovaria."

Rone nodded solemnly. That did sound like a great idea. The problem was, the battle strategies they used to deal with defending themselves would need to be very different than the strategies they would use in offensive maneuvers.

The Captain interrupted his thoughts by saying, "I can see that you're thinking First Sergeant. Please share, you were selected because you're highly successful in combat and that knowledge is key to our success."

"Yes sir."

He cut Rone off by stating, "The regular structures of rank aren't necessary here. What we're doing is going to require a stronger relationship than Officer and Troop. When it's just us call me David."

Rone nodded at him before saying, "I understand. I was thinking that we're going to have to develop new techniques to make an offensive push. Forming up into defensive positions against orcs is great to hold your ground but charging into battle against them like we do against goblins will only cause us to lose the fight."

The Captain then asked, "So what do you think we should do?"

"While the orcs aren't as dumb as they seem to be, I would say we could trick them into an overwhelming trap to crush their numbers. We've been using defensive strategies for so long they should fall for a classic ambush with double flanking."

"I like it."

Rone assed, "We would need massive numbers and it would have to be set up stealthily."

"Massive numbers because they always come in large groups?"

"Also, they are much physically stronger than we are, one on one. So we'd have to overwhelm them in numbers to crush their force. If we don't remove their main force it would be impossible to push them back."

The Captain nodded before asking, "And goblins?"

"I hate fighting them. Instead of waiting for them to come out to attack a village we should find their villages and return the favor. I've never found a goblin village like orc ones so I've always wondered where they lived. My only guess would be caves."

They finally arrived to the South Gate. The Captain gestured over to the left and through a door that was set into the wall itself. These doors usually led up to the tower on each side. Rone went through the doors and out onto the wall. It was where he suspected this fortification would be. He was proven right when he spotted a newer looking addition to the wall. It was almost a whole two story building placed onto the wall.

The Captain stepped in front of Rone and then started walking towards the building as he said, "Our offices consist of two stories. The first floor is a large planning room where we will have our meetings to work on the mission. On the second floor are offices for all of our team. This team consists of six individuals with high levels of experience in the fields that we'll need. You're the man with the combat experience against our direct foes. I'm the commander of our team. We've got a logistics officer who will manage the supply planning, an engineer for the planning and design of our future fortification, an explosives expert who will help us with adding a little spice to our combat planning and best of all we've been assigned a war-mage from the Wizard's college in the capital."

Rone nodded. It sounded like a good team. Maybe the explosives might just be a good way to deal with goblins, if his cave theory was right. He was thinking that really the biggest problem might be dealing with whatever was causing the random undead to crawl down from the mountainside to attack villages. He had no idea what sort of magic or being could resurrect the dead as monsters. It would be something that he would bring up with the war-mage that the Captain mentioned.

As they entered the planning room a voice called out, "Hey David, you finally got our combat guy?"

Rone looked at the man speaking. He was wearing a thick leather tunic and old-looking leather pants. Having off his tunic was a pair of suspenders that had pouches hanging from it. His light brown hair was loose, slightly long, and unkempt. He had brown eyes and a stubble on his face. Rone guessed that he was slightly under 30 years old.

The Captain responded, "We got a Golden Cross winner."

A female voice interrupted, "Whoa you got him? I thought he kept saying no to promotions."

Rone looked over at the female voice. She was an older woman, maybe in her early forties, with long black hair that was tied into a ponytail. She was wearing the long flowing light green robes with golden etching around the neck that flowed to the front of her chest into an unusual swirling pattern. She was the war-mage that the Captain had mentioned.

The Captain chuckled before stating, "He's about to get married so probably needed more money for a family."

Rone casually glanced around the room. He spotted one other person, who was sitting in a chair in the corner away from the door. It was a strong looking young man wearing the military wine-red tunic, black trousers, and sandals. He said nothing.

The Captain turned to Rone and said, "First Sergeant Rone Millar, this is Magess Maritka Rennil."

He gestured at the woman.

"It's nice to meet you." Rone told her.

The woman grinned before stating, "Usually when people see a war-mage, they look either impressed or scared. It's not a surprise you'd seem casual about my presence."

Rone grinned at her while commenting, "A few years ago our platoon was assigned to work with a war-mage to help deal with an orc shaman and his group. He was quite effective."

She reached out a hand and he shook it.

The Captain pointed at the man wearing the leather tunic and stated, "This is Justinian Ironia. He's an expert in explosives."

Rone offered his hand, which Justinian shook, before stating, "Nice to meet you as well."

"Same. We're gonna put a hurting on the beasties."

The Captain then gestured to the silent man sitting in the corner and said, "That's Leftenant Marius Werrin. He's our logistics man."

The man said nothing but gave Rone a nod. Rone took it as a hint that the man was not a social person and simply nodded back at him.

The Captain then stated, "Don't mind him. The Leftenant is a man of success but not much for conversation. Our last man is Staff Sergeant Hanur Johnston. He is our engineer. Right now, he's out working with the engineering battalion to plot out what we'll need. He's not really necessary for the earliest phases of our work but he'll be key once we start working on building our mountainside fortress."

Rone nodded at him. It made sense. The Captain went over their earlier discussion with the group and it was clear that they needed Rone's experience in combat to really put together the group.

He was curious about the undead thing so he turned to the war-mage and asked, "The only thing I'm curious about is what causes the dead to rise again. We've got an issue occasionally with them wandering through southeast villages on occasion. It would be nice to rid them from our people's lives."

The woman answered, "Undead are summoned by necromancers, who are magic users that use the dark arts. Based on the reports I'd say there is a necromancer of very limited skill somewhere out in that mountain range. I'd say he or she is a low priority right now but sooner or later we'll have to find and deal with them."

Rone nodded. That would be something to deal with for certain. The Captain gestured to a large table in the center of the room. Rone walked over to it and looked. It was a map that seemed to be built up like a miniature terrain version of the mountain range. It was very impressive looking. He spotted small figures sitting on it that must have represented different units.

The Captain grinned as he asked, "Do you like it?"

Maybe his facial expression was obvious as Rone looked at the map.

He chuckled before stating, "I do."

"It took months to map out the mountainside enough to make it as close to real as possible. It's some of Sergeant Johnston's finest detail work."

Rone nodded but said nothing.

The Captain changed the subject, "I want to send out some scouting teams, each with one of us in them. We're going to see if we can spot the orc villages for our map and then deal with them as they appear."

"That sounds like a good plan to me. I've found a few villages myself but most of them were just women and children."

"Our goal there is not to kill women and children but we will try to push them out of their villages and hopefully off our mountainside. The plan would be to push on their flanks to force them to the mountain pass."

Rone nodded before commented, "Maybe start off being very loud as we approach and then once they flee we could burn the village to the ground?"

The war-mage interjected, "I can provide a lot of loud but harmless fireworks that might just do the trick to send them fleeing."

"That sounds good." Rone said.

"Well, there is not much else we can do today. I'll coordinate the scouting units for tomorrow and we'll meet at first light. I'll see you all tomorrow."

"Yes sir." Rone said.

He was quite pleased both with the new assignment and the short day. He would have plenty of time before going to see Marah's family.

Chapter 12

After leaving Rone decided it was time to buy the bracelet that a man would offer to a woman once her father accepted his proposal for marriage. Traditionally this bracelet would be nothing but a simple silver bracelet since most men in the Kingdom were not wealthy. Rone decided to go with a gold one since he had more money than most men due to his savings. Especially with his recent promotion he had more money to spend as needed. It came in a small pouch, which he tucked into a pocket to keep safe. He stopped at a shop to buy a bottle of wine. His mother had taught him that it was always polite to bring a bottle of wine when you were an invited guest for supper. He went back to his quarters to change into civilian clothing since it was not appropriate to wear his uniform. Since there were probably a few more hours before he had to head off the Marah's home he decided to check on the home he bought for them once they were married. He was pleased that the home was located a brief walk away from the South Gate. It meant that he could easily visit Marah for lunch almost daily and the trip to and from work would be quick. A quick walkthrough of the empty home let him know everything was fine.

As he stepped out of the home and started to lock it, he heard a voice say, "First Sergeant?"

He turned around to see it was Sergeant Clarke from his last unit. The man looked pleased to see him. Rone grinned at him and extended a hand for him to shake.

As he took Rone's hand he said, "Congratulations on your promotion."

"Thank you Sergeant. I felt bad to leave you men but

since I'm about to be married I figured it was time to get out of the field and earn a little more pay."

Sergeant Clarke leaned closer before asking, "Is it true that you're courting the General's niece?"

Rone chuckled before answering, "Yes. I guess he wanted to find a man he felt she was worthy of so they tricked me into meeting her. Turned out she's both lovely and quite pleasant to be around. We realized immediately that we liked each other."

"Very nice. Normally I'd think a man in your position didn't earn what he has but I've seen bleed with us Sergeant. The men miss you but they're happy for your success."

"I miss serving with all of you as well. With my upcoming marriage I felt I could not refuse the offer for promotion since it might be the last one that I receive."

Sergeant Clarke nodded thoughtfully before announcing, "Well, I must head off. It was a pleasure serving with you."

Rone grinned at the man before replying, "It was a pleasure serving with you."

He watched as the man strode away before deciding to go ahead and head off to Marah's home. Every time he mounted his horse to go to her home he found himself quite happy. The weather was pleasant and maybe it was his own mood but he felt like everyone around him was as joyful as he was. He rode along thinking about what he was going to be doing soon. Since there was no doubt that her uncle would agree to his proposition, he was about to be engaged to be married. Usually these engagements lasted a few weeks to prepare for the simple ceremony and ensure any family who wished to be there would be able to arrive in time. It also gave him time to start purchasing furniture any anything else they would need in their home. His goal there of course was to let Marah pick what she felt comfortable with since she would be spending more time than he would be. His mind wandered about while he rode, and it was not long until her home came into view. There was no one standing outside. It was odd because usually Marah would be waiting for him. Shrugging it off, he dismounted his horse and tied it's reins up. The 'Open' sign that was usually on the door, was not there. Pulling out the bottle of wine that he brought, he knocked on the door. After a moment the door opened to reveal Henri.

Rone said, "Hello."

Rone chuckled as Henri gestured inwards with his head. A man of few words. Rone stepped through the door and waited as Henri closed it. Once Henri started walking, Rone followed him. All this time Rone had never been past the small area that served as Marah's shop. The main area of their home, which was much bigger than Rone had realized, was set up as a dining room with a long table surrounded by several chairs. The smell of some sort of roasting meat wafted to his nose. Off to the right was a large kitchen area where a woman stood working behind a stove. He assumed she was Marah's aunt. She was wearing a plain looking light green dress that was belted by a darker green sash. Her hair was a light blonde color, very close to his own in color, and it was tied into a loose bun on the back of her head. She glanced over at him and he saw she had light green eyes. His best guess was that she was maybe ten or so years younger than the General but old enough to be Henri's mother. Forty or so. He was not the best at guessing the ages of people older than himself.

"Hello Rone." Marah said happily.

He turned to her and grinned before saying, "Hello."

She looked quite lovely in her near white dress that was decorated from across the left shoulder with some sort of golden thread that shaped into a series of flowers embedded in a wreath of leaves. It was quite intricate and probably took her a long time to make. He suspected this dress she had made specifically for the occasion at hand. Her bright orange hair was braided into one long braid that was loosely setting along the back of her head. The General himself was sitting at the position of authority at the end of the table.

Knowing it was polite to always give the formal greeting and bottle of wine to the man of the home, Rone walked up to the General and offered the bottle before saying, "Sir. Thank you for the kind invitation into your home."

Standing from his seat, the General accepted the bottle as he replied, "Thank you Rone. Please take a seat next to Marah."

The General set the bottle down on the table before sitting down.

"Yes sir."

Rone walked over to where Marah was and took a seat next to her. As he looked into her eyes, he gave her a wide grin.

Settle a plate down on the table, which was filled with lamb chops, Marah's aunt said, "It's about time I meet the young man who's trying to steal away my little girl."

Rone looked up at her. She had a smile on her face, which told him that she was speaking in jest.

"It's nice to meet you ma'am." Rone told her.

"And you as well Rone."

Rone thought for a brief moment about when was the right time to ask the General for permission to marry Marah and he realized immediately that the man clearly respected boldness. He decided the time to act was now.

"Sir. Instead of wasting time, I just want to ask directly for permission to marry your niece."

The General chuckled heartily. Marah looked surprised he would just come right out with it but Rone felt there was no reason to wait.

After he finished laughing the General commented, "Much more bold than when you came to my office young man."

"Confidence sir." Rone stated honestly.

He felt much more confident now than he did when he first approached the General looking to court Marah. The answer here was going to be yes.

"Indeed. My question is, before answering, do you understand the importance of what you're asking?"

"Yes sir, I do."

"Let me remind you."

"Yes sir."

"Taking a wife is much more than just simply moving in with her and getting nightly fun in the bed. You're going to be responsible for her safety."

"I understand sir."

"It's more than that young man. You must protect her physically, mentally, and spiritually. You will have to lead her through the hardest of times, whenever they may come. Her honor will become your honor and your honor will become hers. Marah is a kind young woman and I'm confident that she'll be the best of wives so you'll be expected to be the best of husbands. Do you promise to be all of that?"

Rone understood completely what the General was saying. Being married was a burden of a family placed upon a man.

He knew she was the one for him, so he stated firmly, "I do promise sir."

The General brought his hand up to his beard and gently stroked his fingers along his chin. Rone recognized it as a pause for him to set himself as the center of the conversation, a power move. It made him wish he could grow a proper beard as well. Maybe as he aged.

He finally took his hand away from his beard before stating, "Very well. I give you permission. I'll have my wife coordinate the efforts to set up the ceremony."

Rone turned towards Marah and pulled the small pouch holding the bracelet that she would wear signifying their relationship. She must have realized immediately what he was doing because her face lit up. He opened the pouch and pulled out the bracelet. She extended her right arm, which he then attached the bracelet to her wrist.

She told him, "It's pretty. I promise to be the dutiful and faithful wife worthy of your honor."

"I know. I'm glad you like it."

Henri, who had not spoken the whole time asked, "Why isn't it silver as tradition calls for?"

Shrugging Rone answered, "I felt that gold looks better with her skin than silver would."

Marah interjected, "It does. I love it Rone, thank you."

Her aunt suddenly declared, "Well, now that we've got that out of the way, let's eat supper."

Chapter 13

Rone woke up the next morning and quickly got ready. Today he was going to tag along with a scouting team to help find orc villages along the mountainside. First, they would likely have a briefing to plan out where each team was going and then break off into groups. Rone confidently strolled through the town, saluting people as he went, before he finally got to the building on the wall where his new office was. The others were waiting there. The only exception was the last man of the team. He was a much younger man than the others, maybe the same age as Rone. He had neatly trimmed military cut brown hair and dark brown eyes. His skin was heavily tanned from being outside a lot. Like every other military man, he was wearing the uniform.

Captain Bainbridge saw Rone enter and said, "Ahh First Sergeant. We're all here. First, let me introduce you to Staff Sergeant Johnston."

Rone looked at the man and stated, "A pleasure."

The man grinned at Rone before replying, "Thank you First Sergeant. I'm excited to serve with you."

"Right, back to the task at hand." The Captain said before turning to the table-map and gesturing at it.

He then continued, "I've requested scouting teams at six locations for each of us to work with. Once each of you gets there, the plan is to work with your team to scout up the mountainside in the zones marked below. We've had maps printed for each section so we can mark any orc villages. If you spot a village, mark its size and do not engage or interact with them. If they attempt to engage with you, retreat quickly. We don't want injuries and we don't want to trigger a response."

Rone nodded and examined the map. Next to each squad was a small piece of paper with the name of the unit and the name of their team who would be with them. He was mildly disappointed to see his assignment was right up the middle with a completely different unit than his own. It made sense to send Rone up the middle since he had the most fighting experience of the team. He would have loved to spend another day or so with his men. The unit he was meeting with was the 'Green Dragons' Platoon. Rone had heard good things about them but generally knew little.

"Any questions?" The Captain asked.

No one responded so the Captain announced, "Head out. Remember you're not in charge out there, the Officer in charge of the squads you're working with are. Each of us is there is merely there to observe and track. Take your maps and go."

Rone nodded and collected his map.

As they started to head off the Captain called out, "Rone, come here for a moment."

"Yes sir." Rone responded while turning back to the Captain.

"Those orders were for the others. I've let your squads know that if you give an order they're to follow it immediately. I'm sending you right up into the heart of orc territory so it's important they have the best man in case of a situation."

"I understand sir." Rone said.

The Captain nodded before declaring, "Let's go."

Rone turned back to the door and headed off. The only good part about his assignment was the fact his meeting point was not far south of the gate. The others would have to travel for a while before getting to their meeting points. Rone mounted his horse and headed through the gate. Almost as soon as he exited town he spotted about twenty or so men milling about. They were all wearing the traditional military uniform. Many times a unit would come up with a sash or some sort of marker to make their men stand out in a crowd. Rone never had his men do that because he really did not care about that sort of thing. Whomever the man in charge of these troops was had them wearing a green pin on their collar right below their rank. As he rode up to the group he was able to see that the pin was a head of a lizard creature, what he always guessed a dragon would look like. He had heard tales of such creatures way up in the northern part of the kingdom but thankfully they did not exist anywhere near their town. It was enough to deal with hordes of orcs, swarming goblins, and the occasional undead attack. Adding massive building-sized flying lizards was not something he wanted in his life.

As he dismounted a Leftenant approached him and saluted before saying, "Good morning First Sergeant. It is an honor for the 'Green Dragons' to serve with you today."

The man was wearing the same uniform with the green dragon pin as the others. Since it was a scouting mission the men there only were wearing a simple helmet to protect their head and no other armor. Speed was key. Rone could not see his hair since he had a helmet on but his eyebrows were brown so he guessed the man had brown hair. He was clean-shaven and had dark brown eyes.

Giving the man a polite smile, Rone returned the salute before stating, "Thank you Leftenant, it is my honor to serve with you and your men. Do you understand the mission?"

The Leftenant answered, "Yes. We're going to split our scouting teams into groups of four and slowly work our way up the mountainside at a distance of a league or so that will allow us to barely spot each other but enough distance to allow to cover much of the mountain. Our goal is to identify enemy encampments or villages and then withdraw and report them to the lead team that will consist of you, me, and my senior Staff Sergeant. I was informed that you had a map so we can mark enemy positions. We're to withdraw from any potential engagement and if possible we will circle around identified locations to continue traveling up. Finally, we'll form up as the mountain becomes impassable along our spread before our final stop at the mountain pass. From there we'll head back here and that will complete the mission. Am I missing anything?"

Rone shook his head. That was a solid plan. The Leftenant gestured to his left and right as he called out orders to his men. Rone appreciated the efficiency of the men as they moved slowly up the mountainside. He dismounted and left his horse with the troops who were staying near the gate to guard them. It was going to be a long walk up the mountainside. He was kind of glad their path would be one of the least rough of the entire mountainside.

As they began the walk up the mountain, the Staff Sergeant of the unit he was with said, "First Sergeant, its real honor to be serving with the only living winner of the Golden Cross."

Rone looked over at the man. He was in uniform and wearing a helmet too. His eyebrows were a light blonde color and he had blue eyes. Rone guessed that he was a few years older than Rone was.

"Thank you." Rone told him sincerely.

"First Sergeant I've heard rumors how you were awarded it but I was wondering if you could tell me what happened."

Rone nodded. This was probably the one story he was asked more than any other. It was actually surprising to him that Marah did not ask. He could only guess that she did not ask because it was not something she cared or wondered about. Combat after all was a man's work not a woman's.

"A few years ago, I was a squad leader for the Sharp Talon's platoon. Our squad was sent out to serve as a lookout and flanking for the main platoon as it moved to strike a goblin horde moving down the mountainside to a small village named Hardcastle. From our position we could see the goblins moving in on the platoon. Right as they met in combat a second force, this time orcs, moved onto the field and towards the platoon from the flanking side. Their numbers were easily twenty times the number of men in my squad."

Rone stopped so the two men listening as they walked to gauged the danger of the situation. They both looked enthralled as they listened to him talk.

He continued the story, "Since it was our job to protect the flank, I let the men in a surprise strike on the side of the orc's flank since they had not seen us. It was mostly successful at first however the orcs turned on us. Thankfully as they surrounded us, I spotted their leader. Usually you can force an orc retreat if you can take out their leader so I charged out of my weakened formation and forced the leader into individual combat. I was injured in battle but was able to defeat the brute. The orcs withdrew without their leader but as they fled my squad was reduced to four men, all of which were seriously injured with only two of us being able to fight. The goblins were holding their own against our platoon and I spotted our Captain being attacked directly by a retinue of goblins led by an ogre of all things. I left my surviving men behind in a safe spot before I ran to our Captain and engaged the goblins from the rear. As you know goblins are cowardly, which is why most need a much larger beast to lead them without them fleeing at any form of strong resistance. Most cowered and I was able engage the ogre from behind. It didn't see me coming so I jumped onto its back and stabbed my sword into the back of its head. It fell on its side, trapping my left leg under it. Without the ogre to push them forward the goblins fled. Thankfully I only sustained an addition broken leg but we won the day and I was rewarded with the Golden Cross and a field promotion to Staff Sergeant."

The two men looked impressed. Rone had to admit that he got very lucky at every point. He should have been dead three or four times over in that battle.

"Quite a story First Sergeant." The Leftenant stated.

"Indeed. I Should have been dead many times over, but I got lucky."

The Staff Sergeant chuckled as he commented, "Quite modest too."

Off to their right Rone spotted some smoke lazily drifting from a nearby field behind the woods. He could not see what was there but none of their men would start a fire on the mountainside. No doubt it was likely either an orc village or encampment. The two men with him look at each other before looking at Rone and nodding. Rone swirled his fingers to let them know to silently follow him. They nod at him and the three headed off. He moved as cautiously as he could, trying to keep quiet as they crept along the edge of the forest. Step by step he tenderly moved until they could finally see what was there. It was not an encampment nor a village but a small group of orcs. Rone pondered what to do about it. They were there to find settlements of the orcs. He tilts his head to the others, and they slip away. It was probably better to mark the location and move on.

Once they got back to the road Rone announced, "We'll keep moving. Orders are not to engage the enemy."

The Leftenant nodded. He wanted to deal with the orcs to be honest but he knew it was not wise to mess with the Captain's orders. They continued along to the pass smoothly. Once there, they settled down and started a fire to keep warm since the pass was higher up in the mountains. Eventually all of the teams showed up and they briefed each team to get a full setup. The mission was successful and multiple villages were discovered. Rone was not surprised to see the village he had found with women and children in the past was still there. It was nice to see that each team noted what they found. Once the briefing was done, the whole group headed back down the path to town.

Chapter 14

Rone was enjoying his new assignment. He found the bounce back between the team members interesting due to the unique personalities of everyone involved. It was the next day, and he was released for the day. It appeared that this assignment would allow him more free time than normal. The report given to the Captain was effective in giving a very good idea where their enemies were encamped. The plan coming forward would be to form up units to push away these camps through overwhelming numbers. Rone examined the full map with estimated numbers and felt the best strategy was to hit the largest numbered forces first so they could overwhelm the weaker ones later. It was a bit of discussion of this strategy before they decided to send their report up to the higher levels of command for a decision. He decided to pay Marah a visit since he had nothing else to do. Maybe he could take her on a pleasant walk. It dawned on him that he would need to communicate with her to find out what she needed in their future home. The ride to her village was pleasant and when he dismounted in front of her home, he saw the usual 'Open' sign on the door. Rone really was beginning to like the work shifts for his new position. No doubt long days would come once the battle plans they put together were approved. For now, he would enjoy the free time.

As he opened the door to her home, Marah called out, "Rone!"

He grinned at her. Today she was wearing a light blue dress that had white swirled embroidery that started on the top of her shoulders and circled downward on the sleeves. Her hair was tied into a ponytail.

"Hello." He told her while grinning.

She walked up to him and held tightly into a hug.

"What brings you here?" She asked.

"We've sent our plans up to the command and since it will probably take a week or two before the plans can be approved so I've got a lot of free time for a bit."

Marah announced, "Wonderful. Can I finish this little project that I'm working on? After I'll make us some lunch and we can go for a picnic."

"Of course." He replied.

She let go of him and then walked back to where she worked at. Rone took a seat down on the chair he had sat in many times before. She immediately got to work. He was not sure what it was she was working on but it was a large light blue piece of cloth. The best guess he had that it was a dress or maybe something for a table. Rone was horrible with clothing. As she worked she had that look of concentration that she would occasionally get while sewing away. It made him chuckle when she would stick her tongue out slightly while focusing intently on one part or another.

"Marah."

She continued working as she responded, "Yes?"

"Were you planning to open up a seamstress shop once we settle down in town?"

Looking up from her work she answered, "I love doing this but I think I'm going to concentrate on starting our family first. Maybe as our children get older."

He nodded before asking next, "How many children do you want?"

Giving a laugh she responded, "As many as I can. I adore children. Sometimes I do babysitting when mothers in the village have to go to town for shopping."

Rone nodded. It was a subject he did not think about but he knew he wanted his own children, especially a son. The idea of growing a young boy into a man that he molded to someday become a warrior like him greatly appealed to him. After Marah finished her work she excused herself and walked into the main area of her home. Since it was not appropriate for a man to walk into a woman's home without a family member there and without permission, Rone stayed seated. It was a bit of a wait before Marah returned with a basket. He suspected she had packed a meal. Wrapped over her head was a white shawl, likely to protect her skin from the sun since Rone did not bring an umbrella.

"Shall we go?" She asked.

"Of course. Where are we headed?"

"A bit to the east there is a small orchard with plenty of trees that are open enough for us to have a real nice picnic without me getting burned from the sun."

Giving out a little chuckle Rone commented, "We'll have to buy a few umbrellas once we settle in town."

Marah laughed while commented, "I appreciate that."

He gestured towards the door leading out into the village. Marah placed her hand on the back of his wrist and he slowly guided her out of the home and into the village. He had spotted the orchard in question several times during his ride through the village a few times. It was not a far walk south through the village and then east.

As they started to walk Marah asked, "When would you be free for us to shop for everything that we'll need in our future home?"

"I'm free until the orders are either approved or rejected."

"Will tomorrow work?"

"Of course." He answered with a grin.

She smiled kindly at him. He really greatly enjoyed her company. As they approached the village's small central market Rone noticed a crowd was forming up. He had no idea what is going on.

As they began to pass the crowd to head east he heard a voice call out, "Halt."

Glancing at the voice, he saw the man was looking at them. The man was an older officer of the military wearing the military tunic, black trousers, and sandals. The man had dark brown hair that was neatly trimmed and a short beard. Rone caught the man's eyes and looked at him curiously. Since Rone was technically off duty and was wearing civilian clothing, he had no idea why the man stopped them.

"Join the crowd." The man stated.

Shaking his head at the man, Rone stated, "We're heading to a picnic. Thank you for offering."

The man chuckled at Rone before declaring, "This isn't optional. The Royal Mage's Guild is looking for potentials."

Rone grunted. The Mage's Guild sent out people looking for new members regularly since magic was the only way to deal with the monsters that regularly attacked the kingdom from the north. Everything from common goblins like they dealt with here to massive dragons that would spew flames. Rone was quite glad he would not have to deal with the same problems of the north half of the Kingdom. He just shrugged at the man. This was probably the seventh or eighth time he had stood there while the mages recruiting others would wiggle their fingers at the crowd. It left Rone knowing that he had no magical abilities, something he was quite happy about. The man turned away from them and then gestured towards another man. This man was clearly one of the mages. He was wearing a long flowing white robes that had golden stitching in the form of some kind of unusual circular crest. In the middle of the crest was a complex looking flower. He knew that it was the Mage's Guild crest.

Marah whispered in what sounded like a nervous tone, "Rone, I really need to get away from here."

He replied, "Its fine. These dumb mages will cast their silly spell and then we'll be on our way."

"No. I have to leave. Please."

Rone was very confused about this. Why would she be worried about having some magical identification spell being cast on the crowd?

Before he could respond to her insistence on leaving the mage cast his spell. The mage looked around in the crowd and then his eyes stopped on Marah. He gestured towards her. Rone looked at her and her expression was one of extreme nervousness. She was even more pale than normal.

"Her." The mage announced while his hand was still pointed at her.

Rone frowned. Having his soon to be wife identified as a mage was a nightmare. The Mage's Guild would simply seize anyone they find with potential and then send them off to the Capital for training.

Marah released her hold on his wrist and started to step back as she said, "Rone?"

The first man who had called them to the crowd started to walk towards Marah with three other military men. It was obvious that they intended to take Marah right away. Rone stepped between the men and Marah.

He announced, "It is not appropriate for four men to try to hold a lady in such a manner. Perhaps you should find a woman mage to escort her? Especially since she's the niece of a General."

The men stopped walking. He guessed that they realized the precarious situation that they had placed themselves in. Dealing with a relative of a General was always a sensitive situation.

"Call out Magess Illena." The mage announced.

After a few moments a female wearing the same white robe approached the group. She had dark brown hair that was tied into a pony tail and brown eyes. She looked to about the same age as Rone. He was not pleased with all of this. It was going to be very hard to explain to the General how he let these mages take his niece. In reality the laws of the Kingdom were clear. The Mage's Guild had full authority to take any citizen into possession of the Guild if they felt that citizen had magical potential.

"You called Master Pauls?" The young female mage asked.

"Escort this potential to the holding tent. She is to be taken to the Mage's Guild tomorrow where a full magical examination will confirm if she has enough potential to become a member of the Guild."

"Yes Master."

The woman took Marah by the arm and started to pull her away. Marah looked very upset and Rone knew that she did not wish to go with them. He wanted to fight them but it would be a disaster. The only possible option would be to have her Uncle, the General, fight the situation.

"Rone?" She nervously asked.

"I can't do anything Marah."

The male Mage asked, "Who are you to her?"

Rone replied, "I'm her future husband."

The mage chuckled before stating, "Maybe. You may visit her this evening before we take her to the Capital."

Rone nodded firmly. He would have to go to speak to the General right afterwards so the General can work towards getting Marah's release. He watched as Marah was taken away. Her eyes looked quite sad. This would not stand for Rone. He would have to do something as soon as possible. He ran back to her home and found that no one was there. It would have to be after he visited Marah that he could inform her family. He decided to go and see her immediately. As he walked back to the town center, he spotted a nearby open field where the Mages had set up their tents. Confidently he strolled up to the collection of tents and asked a guard where they were holding Marah. There was a pair of guards at the tent entrance but overall the whole encampment was very lightly guarded. It was not a surprise since they were deep within the Kingdom and far from danger.

As he entered the tent in question Marah called out, "Rone!"

She raced into his arms and hugged him tightly. He ran his hand along the top of her head before circling his arms around her. As he glanced around he saw a cot, a small table with one chair, and an empty chest. It was obvious that the mages rarely found something with magic since this tent was only meant to hold one person. Marah was alone until he entered the tent.

In a soft voice she stated, "You have to get me out of here."

"Once your uncle finds out I'm certain you'll be freed."

"No." Marah stated firmly before continuing, "It could take days or even a week for that. I need to leave as soon as possible."

"That just isn't likely Marah. I don't have the authority to override the Mage's Guild. When they find someone who might have magical powers that they could train into a mage it usually takes someone as high ranking as the King to release a person."

"I have no magical powers." She stated firmly to him.

"Then why did their spell identify you?"

"If they find out why, they'll kill me."

Rone frowned. This was very unusual. The Mage's Guild did not kill magic users, they trained them to fight for the Kingdom.

"I don't understand." He told her.

"Get me out of here and I'll explain everything." She replied.

"How would I do that?"

She released her hold on him and then looked into his eyes.

As he looked at her she answered, "I don't know but I must escape tonight. I think if I can get home I'll be able to get help."

"They all know who you are Marah. Going back home won't help, they'll just go to your house in the village."

"Not there. My home. Come back tonight and help me escape Rone."

"That's not wise."

"You promised my uncle to protect me. If you leave me with these mages, they'll kill me."

He frowned. She was quite insistent but he was still confused. She was right that he promised to protect her.

"Where would I take you?" He asked.

"I'll explain it later. I promise."

This was quite confusing to him. She should not be in danger with the mages, but she insisted. Surely, she must have had a reason why which he did not understand yet.

Deciding to trust her he replied, "I'll figure something out and come back tonight."

She gave him a soft kiss and he then walked out of the tent.

Chapter 15

Once he left the tent Marah was in, he hurriedly ran as fast as he could to her home. He was hoping that maybe someone would be there for him to talk to. Once he got to the home, he knocked on the door. After a few moments he was relieved when Marah's aunt opened the door.

She initially had a smile on her face but it shifted as she began to look concerned as she asked, "Where's Marah?"

Sighing heavily Rone told her what had happened from when they left the house and up to his return back. Once he finished the story he could tell that her aunt was distraught.

Rone said, "We must let the General know. I'm certain that he can get her released."

Her aunt shook her head at him before stating, "That will take too long. We must get her out immediately."

"I don't have the authority to just get her released. The mages have the authority of the King."

Shaking her head at him she responded, "It doesn't matter. You must break her out tonight."

Rone was shocked. It would be against the law to break her out and it was not like she would be able to go anywhere that they could not find her. If he brought her to his new home or his quarters, he would be the first suspect that they would have. Obviously he could not take her to her home or to the General in town, they would check all of those places. It was all illegal and he was not very comfortable breaking the law.

Deciding to hear what her aunt had to say he asked, "Why?"

"They'll kill her once the figure out why their magicks detected her."

"Why?"

Her aunt frowned before answering, "It's not my place to answer that. You have to go back there and save her."

"And where would I take her if I did? The mages have authority to search all of our homes."

Her aunt's face shifted thoughtfully for a moment before replying, "Where did she say she wanted to go?"

"Her home but they'll just come and search here."

"Rone…" Her aunt answers with a long pause before continuing, "This is not her home. You promised to protect her since she is your betrothed. Free her and then take her home."

"Where is this home?" Rone asked.

He was very confused because he figured this was her home. Everyone had told him that she was an orphan since she was six years old.

"I don't know." Her aunt answered.

"This makes no sense to me." He admitted aloud.

"Do you care for her?"

Scoffing at the woman he answered, "Of course, I'm betrothed to her."

"Then go free her and I'm certain she can explain what you need to know."

Rone frowned. He was getting nowhere with her aunt as the woman kept talking in circles.

"Fine. I'll get her but you must go tell the General what happened. I guess I can take her home, wherever that is."

"Good luck. I'll let my husband know what happened immediately."

Rone spun back around and headed off. If he was going to free her, he would need to make it appear that he had already left in order to draw less suspicion on him. He decided that the plan would be to ride off on his horse and then return on foot to collect Marah. Since he had to mask his involvement he could take her to stay at the old abandoned barn outside Peel near his home. While leaving her there for the night, he could return to his quarters and pretend to be innocent of her escape before declaring he would help search for himself. Since he had not taken much time off work it would probably be quite easy to get a week off work so he could deliver her home and then return back to town. It was not the perfect plan but it would probably suffice. He was finding himself quite dismayed about this whole problem because his relationship with Marah went from something very pleasant to now almost a criminal aspect as she and her family expected him to steal her away from the Mage's Guild. He sighed heavily. After riding his horse out of the village towards Peel, he stopped to wait. It would have to be right after the sun set before he could do anything.

Once the sun finally set he mumbled to himself, "I can't believe I'm doing this."

Rone could not take the main road since it would increase his likelihood of being spotted so he crept along in the fields while crouching to keep out of sight. Thankfully his time scouting came into use here and he was able to make it to the tents of the Mage's Guild. There were still very few guards. Like Rone had noted earlier, it made no sense to have a lot of guards since few would challenge the Mage's Guild and its authority. He was feeling more than a little nervous about this. If he was caught, he would not be able to fend off a mage since their power as overwhelming. Moving like a thief, Rone cautiously snuck along while keeping as low to the ground as he could and staying out of the light of nearby lanterns. He made his way to the tent where he knew Marah was being held. There were still two guards standing by the only entrance. He moved to the side opposite of the guards and tried to pick up the bottom of the tent to sneak underneath it. It was heavily anchored by dozens of spikes. If he wanted to open the tent from the bottom, he would have to dig out several spikes. It was something that would be both strenuous and loud to do that. The only option would be to somehow silently cut the tent to sneak his way in. Since he did not have a knife, he would have to acquire something sharp to do this. Glancing around he spotted a man in uniform standing alone looking out into a field. He was clearly a guard. Rone guessed that he was probably around Rone's age. He had a sword on his hip but that was it. It was going to be impossible to get the sword without having to knock the man out. Sighing inward, Rone crept closer to the man. It was going to have to be a choke hold or a heavy strike to the man's head to take him down. Deciding to hit the man with a rock Rone picked up a medium-sized rock. It would take a precise strike but should not kill the man but give him a serious headache once he awoke. Moving up to the man Rone finally got within strike range. As Rone lashed out, his strike hitting the man directly on the back of his head, the man grunted and fell down. Rone caught him so he would make less noise.

As Rone set him down, he whispered, "I'm sorry friend."

The man had a bleeding cut on the back of his head so Rone pulled out the man's sword and cut off a piece of the tunic the man was wearing and then bandaged the man so he would not bleed out. Rone was not trying to kill him. He brought the sword with him and then towards the bottom of the tent he sliced through it. His first slice let him know that Marah was likely sleeping since all of the candles were out. He used the sword to continue making a small opening and then slipped through. It was dark so he had to wait a moment for his eyes to adjust. He could hear someone's slow and even breathing which he guessed was likely Marah sleeping. Stepping carefully, he knelt down next to Marah, who he could now see in the dark. She was soundly sleeping and she looked beautiful in her sleep to him.

In order to make sure she did not make any noise in her sleep, he reached out with his hand and covered her mouth while whispering, "Don't yell, its me."

She startled awake and instantly had a look of recognition. He released his hand covering her mouth.

Whispering back at him she happily responded, "You came for me."

"Yes, we're making a huge mistake but your aunt demanded I do this."

"What's the plan?"

"Let's get out of here first and then we'll go over that."

She nodded. He helped her sit up and then she reached out and slid on her boots. As she stood, she took his wrist once again. Rone gestured to the back of the tent and then led her to the opening. Once he crawled through, he helped her.

As she stood up he whispered, "You must sneak carefully and crouch. Can you do this?"

"Like I used to do when playing hide and seek with Duarde and Henri."

He nodded and then waved at her to follow him along. She followed closely behind him and it was not long until they made it out of the mage's encampment. They were still in danger of being spotted so he had he continue to sneak along. It was maybe thirty minutes until they finally made it to his horse. Normally he would not expect a lady to ride a horse like a man but they had no time for chivalry since he had to drop her off at the barn and then hurry back to his quarters. He was surprised when she simply accepted help onto the horse and clenched her arms around him tightly. They rode quickly along the road. It was the perfect time of night since no one was out as they rode along the outskirts of Peel. He did not want anyone seeing them together so he did not go through the town. Circling around, he found his way to the abandoned barn. It was still spring so the weather was mild.

As he dismounted he instructed Marah, "Stay here tonight. I'm going to return to my quarters and pretend like I didn't know you disappeared. Once I've been cleared, which should take a few hours tomorrow morning, I'll request leave from my unit insisting that I must search for my future wife. Then, I'll find my way back here."

"Thank you for saving me."

Rone shook his head. He was still very confused about all of this.

He replied, "When I return I'm expecting a full explanation or I'll walk away."

104

Marah's face shifted to shock and then a look of determination.

"I understand." She told him.

"Stay in this barn. Where are we headed so I may pack supplies?"

"It's near the top of the mountain." She answered.

If he was puzzled before, now it was worse. He did not know of any villages near the mountain top. Maybe it was on the other side of the mountain, which was possible since he did not know the area on the other side very well.

"Very well. I'll see you tomorrow."

He leaned forward to give her a kiss, which she responded to by kissing him passionately. Turning away, he mounted his horse and then waved at her. She waved back and then walked into the old barn. He hoped that he was not making a mistake as he spurred his horse to head off.

Chapter 16

Rone paced in his quarters nervously after waking up. He knew it was best to wait for the guards to come to him and since he did not have to be in the office today he would just wait at his quarters. It was not long of a wait before there was a knock on his door.

Strolling over to the door, he opened it and said, "Hello?"

It was not surprising to see a handful of guards, including two mage's guards standing at his door.

"Rone Millar?" A man who clearly looked like the leader of the group said.

"Yes?"

"We're here looking for Marah Taylor."

Frowning with his attempt to trick them he replied, "She's with the Mage's Guild at their tents in Conberry."

"First Sergeant she was there but in the middle of the night someone cut open her tent and she either was taken or escaped."

Knowing he needed to keep up the charade he yelled out, "What!"

"Indeed. We're here to inspect your quarters and the new home that you purchased to ensure she isn't there."

He continued, "You're accusing me of kidnapping my own future wife. I knew I shouldn't have simply handed her over to you. Now she's missing and you're here harassing me."

"We must insist to examine all of your living quarters."

Knowing his plot was still being designed he feigned surrender and let them enter.

As they walked in and began searching he angrily announced, "I'll have the jobs of all the men involved in this incompetence. You better find her quickly or else."

The men finished searching his small room.

As they shuffled out of his quarters the lead man asked, "Can we see the home you purchased next?"

Not wanting to seem guilty he replied, "Its empty but yes I'll take you there."

It was not a far walk to the new home so he led them there. Once they arrived, he unlocked the door and gestured for them to go in. Several men went in and walked around. It was indeed empty, except a few boxes of household supplies he had already bought. Their examination was a quick one. Rone locked the door of the home.

The lead man said, "We'll continue searching for her. Thank you for your time."

Standing confidently Rone stated, "I'll rot in hell before I rely on you buffoons to find her."

Rone spun on his heel and headed towards the South Gate. He was going to first ask for leave and then he would head to speak to the General. Once that was done he would head to purchase a few supplies for a mountain trek and then head to his family home. It was very close to the abandoned barn. Getting leave was quite simple since they were still waiting on the confirmation of their battle plans. He explained his false story to the Captain as to let him know why he was going on leave to look for Marah. The man wished him luck and told him to take a few weeks if needed to find out what had happened to her. His next stop, the General's office, was a waste of time. The adjutant told him that the General was called away on family business. Rone knew right away that the General had went to deal with the issue around Marah. He thought to stop at her home in Conberry but realized adding more stops would slow him down. Next, he packed up a few supplies into a backpack. Usually it only took a few days to get to the top of the mountain and another to get back on the other side where he guessed her village might be. It would be some dried food, a pair of thick fur blankets they could lay on and cover themselves with, a change of clothes, some medical supplies, and some water skins. He also made sure to bring his sword and to change into civilian clothing. Once he was packed and ready to go, he mounted his horse and headed off. As he rode along, he realized that he would not be able to take Marah with the horse very far. He could not ride it on the mountainside and he could not tie it down anywhere since it would put his poor horse at risk of being hurt while he was gone. He named his horse Martis. Rone had been riding it for over three years and he felt his horse deserved better. After the hour plus ride he arrived at his mother's home and tied up his horse before dismounting.

As he entered Mavin raced up to him and called out, "Rone!"

Rone took the boy into a hug before releasing him.

Mavin must have seen his face because he asked, "What's wrong?"

"An excellent question." His mother's voice echoed out.

He looked over at her and forced out a weak grin before stating, "I've got a big problem involving Marah."

Giving a frown his mother responded, "That seems odd. She is quite a pleasant young lady."

Rone nodded before he finally broke down and explained exactly what happened. She took the story evenhandedly.

After he finished the story his mother said, "Its quite unusual that she demanded to be released. You've put yourself in a very dangerous position son."

He sighed heavily. His mother was right as usual.

"I need to get her some food and water since she's been in the abandoned barn outside our farms."

His mother interjected, "And likely in broad daylight there are people who followed you here and would be watching you very closely."

He nodded while blushing. He had hoped that maybe his mother could bring her something.

Before she could say anything Mavin declared, "I'll bring her food and water."

Rone was quite happy to have his brother volunteer. People would not want to follow children around, especially since Rone decided that he would also head out and wander to draw them away.

He told Mavin, "Let me go wander a little bit before you sneak out. Make sure you climb and hide as sneaky as you can be."

"I will." Mavin stated.

"Let me make some food and pack it." His mother said.

Rone waited until the food was ready and then left the house to walk around. He spotted what he thought were a few guards watching him from a long distance. After some time, he returned to the home. It would have to be dark before he could make his move. He realized that he would not be able to bring his horse since it would be too loud to make the move to collect Marah and take off. With nothing else to do, he decided to take a little nap before having to leave. Once he woke up the sun was beginning to set so he got some food for supper and then had his mother pack him something. Rone knew the land so well that he realized he could easily make his way to the barn without being spotted in the dark.

Once the sun was fully set he gave his mother a hug and said, "Thank you mother."

"Your welcome son. I hope you are able to fix whatever problem the young lady has."

He slipped out the back door of his mother's home where it was much darker and very close to the tall stalks of corn his brothers were growing. The corn would make for excellent cover until he was far away from the home and likely the prying eyes of anyone attempting to watch him. He crept along keeping well below the stalks of corn and moving as silently as he could. Right as he got to the edge of the corn field, he heard a loud amount of noise coming from the house. It was his mother and youngest brother Mavin banging pots and yelling at each other. A distraction Rone thought as he quickly dashed from the open spot of the corn field to the side of the barn.

As he entered the barn he heard Marah's voice whisper, "Rone?"

"Its me." He responded.

He heard her moved quickly before he felt her arms wrap around his midsection. He hugged her back.

"So…" He started to say.

She interrupted him by telling him, "I'm sorry that all of this happened."

"Me too. It's time for you to tell me everything."

"Promise me that you'll listen fully and won't hurt me."

He frowned. Why in the world would he hurt her? He loved her and would die to protect her from danger.

Thinking little of it, he responded, "Of course I won't hurt you."

She released her hold on him and then asked, "Do you know what transmogrification is?"

He was confused. It was a word he had never heard before. It even sounded odd to hear.

"No." He answered.

She sighed heavily before answering, "It's ability to change one thing into something else completely."

"So you can transmogrification things?"

Giving a little chuckle she corrected him, "Transmogrify."

"Oh."

"But to answer your question, no, I can't transmogrify things."

"Oh. So why mention it?"

"What do you know about dragons?"

He was puzzled. What did huge flying lizards have to do with her and magic?

"They're huge flying lizards that breathe fire and are evil."

"Just what most people know."

"Is there more?" He asked.

Rone was starting to wonder how a village girl who spent her whole life far away from anything would know about dragons and magic. He would not claim to be the smartest man in the world but this discussion was starting to cause him to become very concerned.

Marah nodded at him before answering, "The dragons you're thinking of are far up north. Both red and green dragons. There are more races of dragons. To the far east in the desert you can find bronze dragons. They're good dragons who try to hide and stay away from others."

Rone frowned. As far as he knew, there was no such thing as a 'good' dragon.

"To the west there is an ocean with large blue dragons that most think of as sea serpents. They are like bronze dragons who wish to avoid others."

He had heard of sea serpents. It did make sense that they would be mistaken for serpents instead of being a dragon if what she was saying was true.

Interrupting her, he asked, "What does this have to do with us?"

"Have you heard of orange dragons?"

Rone shook his head. Most of what she was telling him was new to him. Marah took a deep breath and then slowly exhaled.

Finally, she said, "Even most dragons don't know about orange dragons."

Rone frowned again. What did she mean dragons knowing? Dragons were mindless beasts who attacked for no reason.

He asked, "Are you saying dragons aren't just mindless beasts?"

Marah giggled before answering, "Even goblins and orcs aren't mindless beasts. All dragons are highly intelligent, with some being more intelligent than others."

Wanting to know, he asked, "How would you know all of this?"

She then answered be asking him a question, "Did you know that dragons are all magical creatures?"

He had not thought about but he answered, "I guess it makes sense. I heard that they were huge beasts that could fly and breathe fire. Something that big shouldn't be able to fly."

"Indeed. Although from what I was told dragons can fly because their bones are hollow. The fire breathing is from an organ in their chest. I was told that they can cast defensive spells, which is what makes them so hard to kill."

"Oh. I still want to know how you know all of this." He pressed in a firm tone hoping to finally get an answer.

Casting her glance downward she answered, "Because I'm an orange dragon."

Chapter 17

Rone stared at her in shock. It was a ridiculous claim for anyone to make. She was a petite woman not a huge fire breathing dragon.

He shook his head at her before stating, "Don't be ridiculous. Dragons are huge and you're tiny."

Tenderly taking the edges of her dress, she curtsied and said, "Thank you. I work very hard to keep my figure lean and pleasing to the eyes."

Rone chuckled before stating, "Now, be serious Marah. What is going on?"

"I told you. Remember when I asked about transmogrification?"

"Yes."

"Orange dragons can transmogrify themselves into other beings."

"So you're a huge flying dragon that can breathe fire?"

Marah laughed uproariously and once she calmed down before stating, "No. I'm tiny, I haven't got the physical strength to fly, and none of us can breathe fire."

Rone frowned. She was saying that his future wife was a dragon, the enemies of humankind. It was nonsense and he did not believe it. Maybe she was touched in the head? The idea that his future wife was a little bit off mentally was not something he thought was good. He heard that mental illnesses could be something that could pass down to children. Perhaps he needed to withdraw from the relationship?

She broke through his thoughts by saying, "I need you to take me home."

"Why?"

"I'm too small and weak to make it alone. There are many dangers on the mountainside."

"That's nonsense. There are no villages on the mountainside."

Chuckling she replied, "Because my home isn't in a village on the mountainside."

He was confused again.

She continued speaking, "Our kind live in a village that has been built inside a cave near the top of the mountain to the southwest of here."

Obviously she was not going to let this whole dragon thing be and tell him the truth. He was starting to move past frustration to anger.

Speaking loudly in a firm tone he said, "Marah stop joking around."

Marah frowned at him as she stated, "I'm not."

Rone took a step back. If she was saying was true, then he had no idea how she could appear as a human like she was.

"I really don't understand. You're clearly human, I've felt your touch."

"That's because I am human."

"So why the theatrics?" He asked.

"Transmogrification."

"What?"

"I told you Rone. Transmogrification is the ability to change something from one thing to another."

"So you aren't human?"

"I am but I'm not."

Rone took his right hand and rubbed his temples. He was deeply confused by her words. It was all complete nonsense. How could she be human but not be human?

She must have realized his frustration because she stated, "Orange dragons have the ability to literally turn themselves from what they were born into something else."

"Shapeshifting?" He asked.

"No. Shapeshifting, which elves have magic to do is just a mask. They appear to be something that they aren't. Transmogrification is taking one thing and making it another."

Rone was finally understanding but he did not believe her words. How could a huge dragon turn itself into a petite orange-haired young woman?

"So if you're a dragon why can't you just fly home? Why are you here? Why did you want to marry me? How am I to believe this isn't something but the ramblings of an unbalanced woman?"

She sighed heavily before stepping back to the other end of the barn farther away from him. Suddenly there was a shifting bright light and in her place was a small lizard creature with bright orange scales standing in her place. The creature was maybe two feet tall. It was wearing the same dress that she had on. He stumbled backwards and tripped on something before falling to the ground. It was all true! He was somehow engaged to a beast.

"By the Gods!" He called out.

The same bright light blinded him slightly before Marah was once again. Her dress was slightly askew so she shifted it to fit her properly.

"Well... I..." Rone stuttered out before he started to try and pull himself off the ground.

He felt a sudden urge to try and get away. Once he got off the ground he started to walk away. Marah raced up to him and fell to the ground while clenching ahold of his leg.

"Please Rone, I'm begging. You saw how small I am. I can't make it home alone in either form."

He scoffed at her before angrily asking, "Why don't you turn yourself into a huge flying beast and just go?"

"I can't. Transmogrification can only turn you into something closer to your actual size. I don't understand the magic behind it."

He tried to pull his leg away from her but she clenched onto him tightly.

"Please don't leave me. I've got no one to help me. You can see why the mages would kill me."

"But you're a dragon. You've tricked me into falling in love with you. Why would you do this?"

She was sobbing and tears were streaking down her face as she held onto him.

She told him, "I love you. It's our kind's way. We're not evil like the dragons that humans know of. All of us become humans and live with them, marry them and raise children with them."

He stopped struggling against her tight hold before asking, "How can a dragon have children with a human?"

"I told you Rone. When we transmogrify ourselves we become human. All the way down to our blood. All of us have had many children with humans."

"Have you?" He asked.

She finally released his leg before standing up and stating, "No. I'm just now old enough to wed."

"So you're really seventeen years old?"

"Yes. Its why I'm so small."

"I must leave." He stated firmly.

"Rone." She softly said.

"Yes."

"Please help me. I cannot do it alone."

"Why did you tell me this? Surely you could have asked your uncle or Henri."

"I can't risk asking anyone else for help without putting them in danger and I trust you implicitly."

"How will going home stop the mages from figuring out what you are?"

She nodded at him and then told him, "I think it's because I'm so young. I transmogrified myself into a small child when I was 6 years old. Just now was the first time I went back to a dragon since then. I've spent more time as a human but everything we do grows stronger over time."

Rone turned to walk away and as he took a step away Marah grabbed his hand and then said, "Please help me."

"No. It's all insanity. You deceived me by pretending to be human."

Suddenly she pulled his sword from his sheath and stepped away from him. He was surprised by the movement. Would she dare consider attacking him? He knew even with a sword or as that tiny little dragon she really was that he could defeat her. She took the sword and turned it towards herself.

Panicked he told her. "No, don't hurt yourself."

She backed away even further before asking, "Why does it matter? Without you to help me I'll die either way."

He took a few steps closer.

"Stay back!" She commanded.

"Marah, there has to be a way. Maybe your uncle could help you?"

"Don't you think I've thought of that? They'll be watching him like a hunting bird tracking prey. If I come anywhere near him they'll see me."

"Can't you become someone else?" He asked trying to think of something.

She yelled out, "It doesn't work like that. This is who I am. I don't understand why you can't seem to believe me. I can't shapeshift into anything I want."

"I'm sorry Marah, I'm trying. Its just so hard, you're not human."

"Damn it Rone, I'm just as human as you are right now."

She suddenly took his sword and sliced it across the tip of her right index finger, causing it to bleed.

"Look! I bleed just as you do." She called out while showing him her wounded finger.

Rone walked up and took the sword from her. He looked at her finger. It was indeed bleeding just as his would if he had cut his finger. He was completely befuddled. Reaching out a hand, he poked her finger where she cut it.

"Ouch!" She called out and pulled her finger away.

He examined the spot on his finger where he touched her. It was covered a small dab of blood. It did indeed look like blood of a human. It had the same salty smell, one he had smelled many times in combat. It was very puzzling because if he had not seen her turn into a small lizard he would have not believed her claims at all. He did not believe her until she did so. The fact that he felt tricked really burned at his heart. Something in his mind wondered if any other members of her family were these dragons as well. Thinking about the General being a dragon was stunning. From what Rone had known, the General had served the Kingdom loyally and faithfully for over forty years starting as a young Leftenant. Could Marah be right that these orange dragons were not the same as the dragons he had heard of?

Something about feeling tricked caused his heart to harden so he announced, "I cannot participate in this."

He backed away from her. Upon his announcement Marah's face shifted from obvious nervousness to clear sadness. He was in awe of how realistic the form that she took was with any other human. She certainly kissed him as a human woman. He remembered hearing her heart beating fast the many times they came close to him bedding her. It made him wonder if her claims of being able to bear children was true or not. Marah collapsed to her knees and began sobbing. It made him feel horrible to see the woman that he had so recently declared his love for like this. This whole thing has put his entire life in risk. Helping her escape was likely a catastrophic mistake that could cost him his career if someone were to find out. Worst of all, his honor was stained by all this. Even if no one ever found out, he knew.

Marah continued crying before finally choking out between sobs, "I'm scared. I can't do this alone."

Rone wanted to harden his heart but seeing her like this was hurting quite a bit. She had seemed like a sweet woman and all of this really frustrated him because he knew that she was not actually a woman at all.

She then said solemnly, "I guess I'm on my own."

Slowly she pulled herself up off the ground and began walking towards the door of the barn. Rone wondered how far she could even make it alone. He doubted that she would make it out of the Kingdom before being seized. There was no question in his mind that all guards throughout the Kingdom have been informed to look for her. She would likely be captured immediately and now that Rone knew the truth he could see why she would have been killed by the mages. He frowned because he still cared about her and did not want to see her dead, even with the lies.

As she started to open the barn door Rone announced, "I'll take you home."

Chapter 18

Marah turned towards him when he announced that he would take her and then raced up to him before she started hugging him tightly. He was unsure how to react because their relationship was irreparably ruined. He just stood there as she hugged him without responding.

Once she let go of him she said, "Thank you so much."

Trying not to seem mean he commented, "You probably wouldn't make it out of the Kingdom."

She nodded solemnly. He gestured towards the door and watched as she walked out. He was not going to be able to get the horse so they would have to walk all the way up. An hour ride on a horse while on the main road to town would be an hour and a half but since they had to sneak around towns, it would take all night just to make it to the mountain.

He said softly, "We must walk through the night to take advantage of the darkness. Will you be able to handle that walk?"

Her face shifted to a resolute and grim look as she answered, "I'll do whatever I must do. I'm confident the elders will be able to help me."

"If they can, what will you do?" He asked as they began walking.

She looked thoughtful for a moment.

Her face shifted again to sadness as she answered, "I guess go back to living with my uncle. I believe you a man of honor who would not reveal the truth."

"Not like anyone would believe me." He stated.

She clearly realized that their relationship was over. It made him a little sad thinking about it since he was quite excited about their future together but he could not live with what he knew. He glanced back at his mother's home. It was still dark with only the torch near her porch being lit. Rone had little doubt that the man or men set to watch him were still there watching. He turned forward and kept walking. Marah was not as fast as he was walking so he had to slow his pace so that she could keep up. They had to trudge through open fields for a while before they came across the main road. Rone pulled out a cloak from his pack and passed it to Marah.

"Put this over your head to hide your appearance. We're going to use the main road until sunset. We should be able to make it to the outskirts of town before we have to turn away. You said your home was on the southeastern of the two peaks correct?"

She pulled the cloak over her head to hide her face in shadows of the cloak's hood before answering, "Yes. I barely remember it myself but I was told that it was on the eastern side of that peak."

Rone nodded and kept walking. She followed closely beside him. He was glad that she did not try and hold his wrist like she used to since it would make things even more awkward than it already was. The visual of what she looked like as the lizard looking creature popped into his head. It was interesting that the bright orange hair she had now seemed to be the exact same color of her skin as a lizard. He wondered if it were possible that the reason the area around town had such a larger number of people with orange colored hair was because either so many of these dragons lived there or like Marah claimed, it was the children of these dragons.

He was curious so he asked, "Are the children you have while a human also human or are they like you?"

She answered, "They are humans. They can't transmogrify themselves and most never know that one or both of their parents can do so."

"Both?"

"Yes. Many times two of us become human and live together as humans. Like I have said, when we transmogrify into humans, we're as human as you are. We have children who are human because we're human when we have them."

Rone nodded. It was starting to make much more sense. These dragons would become a human and live like them.

"Why do you do it?" He asked out of curiosity.

Marah chuckled before asking, "Remember that first time we kissed? The feeling when our first lips met."

He grinned. It was one of the more positive moments in his life.

She must have saw his response because she continued speaking, "We can't feel that as dragons. The softness of humans and their physical reactions from each other. I've daydreamed about the stories I was told how being a human was magical. How humans were so wonderful and living as a human was a special experience. I didn't know if I believed it until you kissed me. It was wondrous and had me imagining how much better it was going to be when we finally made love on our wedding night. Our kind live long lives and yet we can't do in our long lives as dragons what humans are capable of doing during their very short ones. Your technology has leapt massively since we first encountered your kind as primitive tribal wanderers using stone tools to survive. I can only imagine how much more you'll accomplish during my life. Being a human is amazing to our kind."

"How long do you live?"

"I was told we can live up to two thousand years."

Rone's jaw dropped. Humans would be lucky to make it to seventy years.

"What of the children your kind have? Do they live that long?"

She shook her head at him while answering, "They're human. They live and die as human."

Rone nodded his head. He thought that he finally understood the whole thing. Part of him wished he could tell someone but he realized telling anyone would make him seem like he was touched in the head. It would only take a few days and since he was on leave he could take her to her home. His mind spun with more questions to ask but he decided to just keep quiet and walk along. They made their way past the nearby villages and the lights from town was starting to come into view. He could see a few people on the road and decided it was time to exit the road so they would not be spotted. While walking through the woods he decided that once they hit the base of the mountainside they would stop and take a break. Marah's pace was slowly decreasing, likely from being unused to walking such long distances. He was really starting to believe that she was right, she would not have made it alone. As they got to the mountainside the sun had come up enough to see the mountains.

Marah pointed at the peak off to the side and away from the usual area that he would take his men on scouting trips before saying, "That's where it is."

Glancing around to make sure no one could see them Rone told her, "Let's take a break here for a while before we begin up the mountainside. We'll need to move along the lowest ridge near those trees making our way to the base of the peak your home is in before we go up. There are several orc encampments once you start up. After we get past the orc encampments we'll have to worry about goblins or maybe even undead."

"How do you plan to deal with any of those?"

"Running. Orcs are slow and cumbersome in rocky terrain and goblins tend to only attack when pressed or if you have food, unless they get an orc or ogre to lead them."

Marah nodded. Rone took out a thick swath of fur and laid it down. He then pulled off his pack and set it on the ground next to the fur.

"Take your boots off before stepping on the fur. We'll need to sleep on it and we don't need mud there too."

"I will." Marah told him as she bent over to unlace her boots.

Rone sat down on the end of the fur and pulled his boots off. After spinning around he opened his pack and pulled out both a water skin and some food.

As he passed some dried meat to Marah she said, "Thank you."

"You're welcome."

They sat there quietly eating and drinking. Rone was so flustered about his situation that he could not think of a way to converse with her. He was half mad at her and also quite curious about the whole thing. He had always thought of dragons as massive evil flying death machines. The creature she turned into was not a death machine of any kind.

Wanting to know he asked, "I've heard stories that dragons grew to the size of several large buildings. Will you grow that big someday?"

She shook her head as she replied, "No. We do not get much taller than any human and I was told it was the reason we got away from other dragons as they would kill us or for some time tried to enslave us. Most dragons are solitary creatures. Our kind used to be but as we've lived with humans we've become more like them. We're now as social as humans and honestly I've always thought that we're more like humans, even as a dragon, than we are like dragons."

Rone nodded. As she explained things it was making more and more sense. She claimed that they were obsessed with humans.

"Let's keep going." He declared while sliding on his boots.

Once Marah got ready he collected up the fur and they headed off. They still had a full day of walking ahead of them and he was feeling a little bit tired already since neither had a full night's sleep. Likely once the sun began to set they would set up a camp. They walked for hours and stopped for a brief break and lunch before continuing. The massive majority of their walk was spent silently walking. It was slowly starting to shift closer to nighttime when they made it to the bottom of the mountain peak that she said they had to go to. It was going to be a real climb up the side to make it there. He did not want to stay with her near the flatter ground since that would be where orcs could wander across them.

"Will you be able to climb the mountainside?" He asked her.

"I'll try my best. When I was a young girl I used to love climbing trees but when I was close to blossoming to womanhood my aunt made me stop since she said it was not a ladylike activity."

Rone nodded before gesturing towards the first small cliff side. Deciding it was best to boost her up, knelt down and patted on his knee to let her know to use his knee to help her up. She smiled at him before stepping up onto his knee with her right foot. As she shifted to pull herself up, he reached out and pushed her upwards. It was mildly embarrassing when he realized he had accidentally grabbed her right on her rear end to push her up. It was the first time he grabbed her rear end and he found it was a pleasant experience.

Once she was up she turned around and said, "Okay, I'm up."

"Take my pack." He instructed her.

She knelt down and took his pack as he passed it upwards. Jumping slightly, he grabbed the end of the small ridge and then using his feet, pulled himself upwards.

As he stood up to brush off his knees she asked, "Are you going to be groping me the whole climb?"

He knelt down so she could make the next climb before blushing at her and saying, "Sorry it was an accident, I was aiming to push you up by the leg."

She set down his pack and then as she stepped again onto his knee commented, "I didn't say stop."

Giving out a chuckle he once again pushed her up the same way. It really was the easiest way to push someone over an obstacle and he had pushed many of his fellow soldiers over obstacles the same way. He found the experience of doing it with

125

her to be much more pleasurable. It only added to the confusion of his situation because he had to remind himself that she was still a dragon, even though her rear felt real and so good to touch. Passing his pack up to her, he pulled himself up the cliff. They only had one last one to go before they could take a smooth walk through a wooded area where he planned to camp for the night since the wooded area would provide them with cover. He knelt once again to help Marah climb. As he was pushing her up, she must have lost her grip because she tumbled downwards at him. Since he was pushing she was shoved slightly away from him and roughly landed on the narrow cliff. She called out in fear by screaming. Rone barely caught her as she bounced off the cliff and began falling off the second ledge. Her facial expression was one of pain and she was clasping her arms where she had landed on her side. Tears began to well in her eyes.

Kneeling next to her he asked, "Are you okay?"

"My side hurts where I landed."

"I'm sorry, I guess I was pushing too hard."

Shaking her head, she stated, "I slipped while trying to pull myself up. Thank you for saving me from falling."

"How bad is it?" He asked nervously.

"It hurts when I breath."

"Do you think you can make it up the next ledge? There is a small wooded area we'll be camping at for the night."

"Yes." She answered.

He helped her rise to her feet and then very carefully aided her in making it up the last cliff. Once he was up, they walked over to the wooded area. He moved into the middle of the wooded area and set down his pack before laying out the fur for them. Taking off his boots, he sat down. Marah sat down next to him. Her facial expression was one of quite a bit of pain. Hopefully her side was not badly injured.

"Let me see your injury." He ordered.

She flushed lightly at him before replying, "Okay."

He had not realized what he was asking her to do until she started to unbutton the top half of her dress. It caused him to blush but it was important to see how badly she was injured. She was wearing a light pink undergarment that covered her bosom but he could see the deep purple on her side where she struck the ground. It was pretty ugly looking.

"This might hurt a little bit but I'll try to be careful checking it."

Her face shifted to a look of resolution. Rone tenderly touched the side where she was bruised. Marah grunted lightly in pain. He touched her soft skin, which he had to admit he greatly enjoyed, and could tell immediately that nothing was broken. Most likely she simply had a deep bruise on her side.

"It's a minor injury. Go ahead and put your top back on."

Marah giggled lightly before saying. "It doesn't feel minor."

He laughed at her joke at watched a little more intently than he probably should have been as she buttoned the top half of her dress back up. He offered her some water and some food, and they ate in silence. Once they were done eating, he pulled out another large swath of fur. It was a lovely night and honestly, he felt like they would not need a fur blanket to keep them warm.

"Let's get some sleep." He told her before sprawling out on the right side of the fur to leave her space on the left side to rest.

She nodded before lying down a little more than an arm's length away from him. He looked up in the sky and enjoyed the night sky. It was beautiful and the stars really looked pretty. Marah shifted to her side with her back facing him. He continued to enjoy the night's sky before he could hear Marah softly crying while she was facing away from him.

"Marah?" He called out softly.

He heard her sniffle and then say, "Yes."

"Why are you crying?"

In a sullen tone she answered, "Those bastard mages ruined everything. You were going to be my first and it was going to be wonderful."

"First?"

She sat up and turned to face him. Her eyes were reddened from crying and she looked miserably unhappy.

"Our kind lives a long time and many of us marry multiple humans and live full lives with them. Of them all, none impact us like our first. The first human we marry and mate with is always the most special. My family back home told me many times about how even as we come close to our final deaths some of our kind call out sadly for their first. They love them even more than their own dragon mate. My father told me that it took him almost one hundred years after his first's death before he would even become a human again. One of my cousins took his own life after his first died because he could not imagine living for centuries without her. I had Uncle Gerrard pick the best man possible because I wanted my first to be perfect. All the things that I told you about how I imagined you would be, were true. I can't imagine any other man being my first now that I've met you."

Rone was flattered by her words.

She continued speaking, "It hurts so much and really is something no one had mentioned how much this emotional pain could be. You've been taken away from me. I see how you look at me now, instead of love, I see anger and even fear."

Rone frowned because that was not his intent. He was just as frustrated and mad about everything that had happened. He had no idea what to say to comfort her.

Giving him what he knew was a fake smile she announced, "Let's get some sleep, we have a long few days ahead of us."

Rone nodded and laid back down again.

Chapter 19

Rone woke up the next morning and was quite surprised that Marah had moved from facing away from him to snuggling tightly up against him. Her head was resting against his shoulder with one arm resting over his chest and one of her legs draped over his leg. He was so tired that he did not notice her move much closer next him. He looked at her resting face, which was peaceful as she was still soundly sleeping. It was lovely at night when they had gone to sleep but the air was now brisk and slightly chilly but not outright cold. Part of him was uncomfortable having her so close to him but another part was quite excited. Dragon or whatever, she sure felt like a fit young woman pressed against him. The sun was barely poking up into the sky and outside of his emotions, he was quite comfortable, so he decided to just let Marah sleep. Since she was unused to walking as much as they had it was probably best to let her get rest. During their long walk her hair was quite a bit frazzled and now she had several long strands of orange hair that were loose and flopped over her face. He tenderly lifted some of her hair off her face so he could see her face fully. She really was beautiful. It was a curiosity whether she purposely made herself look this way or grew into it. The way she described things he was left with impression she became human at a very young age and then aged normally like he did. Either way, she was lovely to look at while lying pressed up against him. Her eyes suddenly opened, and she shifted slightly before looking right at him.

Her face turned red as she said, "Hello."

"Good morning. I hope you're feeling well rested."

"I am. I need to use the restroom."

Giving out a light chuckle Rone pointed over towards some nearby bushes before stating, "I'm afraid you're going to have to rough it out."

"Oh. I've never had to do that."

As she sat up Rone commented, "There's a first time for everything. Remember, this was your idea."

"I know. I'm just a little embarrassed."

Her face turned an even darker red before she almost whispered out, "What do I wipe myself with?"

"Sadly, I think leaves might be your only option."

Nodding at him, she stood up and walked away. After she left, he relieved himself and then started packing up the furs. He then selected some dried fruit and a few pieces of meat for them to eat while walking before slipping his pack on. Thinking about it, he remembered that there was an abandoned hunting cabin on the mountainside about a day away from here. It would be the perfect stopping location for tonight. After a brief wait Marah returned. She looked very uncomfortable.

She solemnly stated, "Remind me never to do this again."

He chuckled. It was well known that women were not meant for rough living.

"How is your side feeling?"

Giving a soft smile in response to his question she answered, "Thank you for asking. It hurts more than anything I've ever felt but it feels better than it did yesterday."

Nodding at her he gestured for them to continue walking. He passed her some of the food to eat. They ate and walked in silence. He could think of hundreds of questions to ask about the whole dragon thing but really, he was more interested in her.

Deciding to ignore modesty he just asked, "What all can you transmogarfy into?"

She giggled lightly before replied, "Transmogrify."

"Sorry, transmogrify."

"Really only sentient beings that I come in contact with."

"Sentient?"

"That means beings with the ability to think and understand basic concepts."

"Why does that matter?"

She paused for what he thought was a moment to think before answering, "I was told that if I did it to become something like a bear or a bird I would be forever stuck as that since I wouldn't have the mental ability to understand how to transmogrify back."

"Ahhh… So, humans, what about dwarves or elves."

"Have you ever seen young boys whitewashing old buildings and then sat there watching the paint dry?"

"Of course not."

She let out a giggle before saying, "That's what I'm told it is like spending 200 years as a dwarf because they're boring and unimaginative."

He chuckled. He had met a few dwarves and he really did feel they were quite dour.

"Elves?"

"Apparently every elf is naturally magical, and they seemed to realize who we are right away."

He nodded.

She then added, "Also, they're really weird with their traditions."

Her comment confused him, so he asked, "Weird?"

Blushing heavily, she leaned closer to him and whispered, "It's not ladylike to talk about it."

Immediately he realized that she was talking about sex. He did hear rumors that the elves were very deviant.

She must have realized that he figured out what she was talking about because she then commented, "As I stated, we've become much more like humans in our culture and beliefs to the point where no one even knows what our kind originally was like before we started living with you."

He nodded. It would make sense that living with someone long enough would change you. They continued walking along in silence. From where they were he guessed that they were just under three days away. They took a brief break for lunch and kept pushing forward. It was probably a good thing that the nearest orc village was over a day away from them, so he felt the likelihood of running into orcs was much less than anything else. As they pressed on, he thought he heard an unusual sound coming from their right. It was not a good thing, especially since he had recognized the shuffling and generally loud movement as likely the undead. Others tended to move silently not to draw attention to themselves. He stopped to listen for a moment.

Marah started to speak but he quickly whispered out, "Shhhh."

Listening intently, he identified that whatever was making the noise was shuffling towards them. It was only one of whatever was there. Finally, he was able to spot what was making so much noise. It was an undead human. Once a man, maybe in his thirties, Rone spotted the shambling rotting corpse as it continued moving in their direction. Its flesh was half rotted and Rone spotted a torn and heavily damaged wine-red tunic and ripped black trousers. It was once a member of the Kingdom's military. Rone could tell that it one time had blonde hair.

Marah must have saw it because she said a little too loudly, "By the gods."

Her voice was laced with more than a little fear and disgust. Rone frowned because she drew the creature's attention. Once the undead got the scent of prey, it was hard to shake them. They moved slowly but they were relentless. Hoping that they would be able to slip away he grabbed her by the hand and pulled her away from it and towards the abandoned cabin. It was still a little bit of a distance and he hoped that they might be able to lose the undead. Rone was thankful that at least there was only one. Sometimes they would come in groups. They walked briskly at first to put some distance in a direction somewhat away from the cabin but enough towards their goal that they should shift directions.

As they walked briskly Marah's voice sounds panicked as she asked, "Was that an undead?"

132

"Yes. We need to get some distance and then try to sneak away another direction."

"How will it know where we went?"

"I'm not sure but the command thinks it's some kind of magic where the undead can sense living humans. They don't seem to attack orcs, goblins, or other animals." He answered.

Rone continued to push the pace as fast as he could with Marah following him. She was nowhere near as fast as he would have liked but it was still fast enough to get distance between them and the undead monster likely following them. As they went, they crossed a stream. Rone hoped that the stream might alter its path following them so that they could escape. He felt that they had got far enough that if they were to lose it, it would be here. He decided to mask their actual direction by turning the path in a few directions. He walked back and forth in several directions and then went back and circled one more time before finally going towards the cabin. They walked for a few more hours before the abandoned cabin came into view. It was pretty rough looking but intact enough to hold for a night.

He pointed at it and told Marah, "We'll be staying here tonight."

"Okay."

"I'm going to leave you here in the cabin for a bit so I can make sure we weren't followed."

"Rone… I'm not comfortable being here alone."

Placing a hand on her shoulder he told her, "I've got to make sure the undead didn't follow us. Let's see if there is a way to block you in safely so nothing can get to you."

She frowned at him but nodded. They walked into the cabin through the door. He was quite surprised by its condition since he expected a nearly destroyed mess, but it must have been a well-built log cabin because it was in solid condition. The cabin itself was virtually empty with only a few slot windows that allowed someone to peek outside without anyone or anything getting in or out. It was just one simple room with space for a bed, a table with a few chairs, and some walking room. Along the back wall of the cabin was a built-in stone fireplace. Almost all the furniture was long gone with only a plank that seemed to be the broken pieces of possibly a table or a shelf.

Flinging his pack off, Rone announced, "We'll use this plank to wedge underneath the handle of the door."

Realizing that she probably would not understand his intention, he picked up the plank and wedged it under the handle of the door.

"You'll need to place plank like this and then stand on the piece where it meets the floor. This will provide a huge amount of leverage that will prevent anyone from being able to open the door without a massive amount of strength but limited effort on your part. Do you understand?"

Marah nodded at him, but she looked quite nervous.

Wanting to give her a little bit of confidence, Rone again placed his hands on her shoulders before telling her, "I don't think that I could push it open doing this. I'll just be gone for an hour or so."

"What if you don't come back in an hour?"

"I will. Just wait here, okay?"

Giving him a nod, Marah answered, "Yes."

Feeling that he should at least give her some reassurance, Rone reached out and gave her a hug. She squeezed a hold of him tightly. Once she let go, he headed out.

Turning to the door he said, "Put the plank in place and just be patient."

He heard the plank of wood click into place. Nodding to no one, he spun on his heel and headed back towards the direction they came from. Without Marah he was able to push his pace much quicker and as he walked he was not surprised that all his effort to trick the undead creature had failed. It was shuffling slowly and steadily towards the cabin. The only option would be to kill it. Rone remembered the only way to do that would be to behead it. He only had his sword, which would do the trick but the undead usually were so aggressive and ignored most injuries. It was still a good distance away from him and slowly plodding

134

its way closer. Rone paused for a moment to make sure no one else was nearby since the last thing he needed was to charge at the creature only to have someone or something else attack him. There was no other sound. He really detested fighting the undead.

Muttering to himself silently he said, "Here goes nothing."

Shaking off his moment of fear, Rone confidently walked towards the undead monster and pulled out his sword. He was planning to make a charge directly at the beast while taking as hard as possible slice at its neck. The plan being of course would be to decapitate it right away, ending the fight. To generate as much power as possible he began running towards it. He could now hear its groan as it must have sensed him approaching. Building up speed, Rone kicked back his sword and swung as violently as he could at its neck. It was a bit of bad luck as it reached out with its right hand and Rone's powerful blow was cut short and defected it slightly. His sword cut through the top half of its hand and got wedged into its head. The creature pushed into Rone and began biting at him. Since his sword was stuck, Rone let go of the handle and then spun away to avoid the biting attack. Its free hand grasped at him and got ahold of the sleeve of his left arm. Its grasp was so strong, Rone was trapped briefly as it pushed onto him and caused them to tumble to the ground. He used the momentum of the fall to spin away from the creature and bounce back to his feet. The creature's grasp on his sleeve was so strong that it caused the sleeve to tear open. He backed away from it and then lashed out with a kick to its head. Somehow it got a hold of his trousers, although the kick did knock his sword loose from its skull.

"Let go!" Rone yelled out as he pulled his leg away from it, which only caused him to stumble to the ground.

He flailed and rolled before finally being able to get away from the creature. Something must have cut or stabbed his back because he felt a slight sharp pain as he hit the ground. Since he had other things to deal with, he ignored it. As he rose to his feet, the creature stood as well. It immediately began moving towards him. Rone circled around it to see if he could find his sword, which he spotted behind it. Moving backwards to draw it towards him, he slowly rotated around so he could pick up the sword. His plan worked perfectly as he was able to collect his sword. This time he decided to slowly cut the thing to ribbons before finally finishing it off. He braced himself to be ready when it came towards him.

"Come here beast!" Rone yelled out.

It groaned before moving towards him. Once it got into range, Robe slashed at it while dancing to his left. He moved again and cut downwards towards its leg. The goal he decided to take was to cut out its legs from underneath it. His slash was successful as he hit a tendon, which caused it to start dragging its leg. Rone dashed off to his right and then took another slash to its other leg. This time he was not as successful and missed his target. The creature slashed at him wildly, which cut into the exposed part of his left arm where his tunic was ripped. Rone swung precisely at the opening its wild swing to strike its neck. His blow was perfect, and the sword cut deeply into its neck, causing the thing's head to lull backwards. Rone lashed out with a kick, knocking the beast down. It twisted and turned in the ground for a moment before it finally stopped moving. Bringing his sword back around, he hacked its neck again to make sure that it was beheaded. The sword was covered in blackish colored blood, so Rone wiped it off on the tunic of the now-dead creature. He decided to burn its body and after clearing the debris around it, he got a fire going and burned its body. The undead were unusual in that they seemed almost flammable so when you would burn the bodies, they burned easily. Rone took a moment to let his sword heat up in the fire to make sure any of the blood of the creature was burned off before he headed back to the cabin. His body was fatigued, and he really needed sleep. It took him a little while before he finally got to the cabin.

Knocked on the door he said, "Its me."

He could hear Marah move the board before the door opened. She opened the door and then ran out to hug him. He half hugged her in response due to his fatigue.

"I was very worried about you." She said before letting him go.

"It wasn't fun. I've got a few minor wounds we need to tend to so that they don't get infected."

In a deeply concerned tone she asked, "You got hurt?"

"Minor scratches, nothing to worry about."

He walked into the cabin and sat next to his pack. It was probably a good thing that he packed an extra tunic to wear. This one was going to be used to bandage his wounds. Marah entered and closed the door behind him.

"Can I help?" She asked.

"Yes please. I fell on a stick or branch that stabbed into my back. I'll need you to pull it out and bandage it once it's out."

Moving carefully, Rone slipped his tunic off. He felt the stick pull out and there was a moment of pain from that point before he just decided to ignore it.

"Your back is bleeding!" Marah called out in a panicked tone.

"It'll be fine." Rone responded before taking his sword and cutting a swath of his tunic off and passing it to her.

He then instructed her, "Press this against the wound. It'll stop bleeding."

She took the cloth and pushed it against the wound. He sat down and cut the tunic into several more pieces. Next, he pulled out a water skin and then poured it on another piece of the tunic and rubbed it into the scratches on his arm. This one he needed to clean immediately to keep it from getting infected from the foul dirty undead's fingernails that had scratched him. Digging in his pack, he pulled out the small vial of ointment the military would issue for infections in the field. He rubbed some of the ointment in the cut and then took another piece of cloth to wrap around it, which he then tied around his arm to bind the wound. He had not noticed it initially but as he sat there, he felt

Marah's very soft free hand gently rubbing his shoulder opposite the wound. It felt very nice.

"Check to see if it's still bleeding?" He asked.

He felt her move the cloth off his back and then she said, "Its stopped."

Rone nodded and then turned around. He felt it was very minor and knew that it would not last long. The sun was beginning to set so Rone decided to stand up and prepare their temporary home. He figured that it would be wise to make it so the door was not able to be opened from the outside. Taking his sword, he cut into the floor to make a notch that the plank of wood stayed in once placed in the notch and under the door handle. After a bit of work and measuring, he got it just right. If someone were to force the door open, they would need a lot of force that would make enough noise to wake him. He then pulled out the fur that they would sleep on and laid it flat. He dragged the pack near the fur and then took a seat next to it.

Since he was still not wearing a tunic he asked, "Could you press the cloth over my wound and then use this last piece to tie it in place for the night?"

"Of course." She answered before picking up the piece of cloth.

Marah took the loose piece of cloth and then wrapped it around his shoulder.

As she worked, she commented, "You're quite fit."

He chuckled because being fit was a requirement in his career field. He would exercise regularly with his men to keep in good shape.

Once she finished, she announced, "I don't think it'll hold while you sleep but maybe it might keep you from bleeding all over the fur."

"That's all I need."

The sun had finally set so Rone shared some food with Marah before they decided to go to sleep. It was a bit chillier, so Rone pulled out the second fur and as Marah laid down, he covered them both with it. She was twitching and fidgeting a bit before she stopped moving while lying about an arm's distance from him.

Her soft voice whispered, "I'm kind of scared, could I rest on your shoulder?"

Since he saw no harm in it, Rone answered, "Of course."

Part of him greatly enjoyed waking up cuddled closely next to him. As she leaned into him, he was shocked when he felt her skin press against his bare skin. She must have removed her dress when she got under the blanket. Her chest felt warm against his and he found himself quite excited. He wanted to say something but lying there with her was very pleasant. Instead of saying anything, he brought his arm around and placed it on the small of her back. He could feel her undergarments on her hip, so he knew that she was not fully nude.

"Rone."

"Yes?"

"Thank you for coming with me. I'd have died horribly without you."

"You're welcome."

Part of him thought of taking advantage of her nudity but he was so exhausted from a long day of walking and combat that he fell asleep holding her closely next to him.

Chapter 20

Sunlight sliced through the slotted windows of the cabin and forced Rone awake. His body was still a little sore from fighting but he was feeling well rested.

As he shifted to move Marah said, "Good morning."

Looking towards her, he saw that she was awake. He could see her bare shoulders poking out from the top of the fur covering them. Her shoulders were just like her face in that they were a light color with hundreds of freckles on her skin.

"Can I ask you something?" She said in a very soft voice.

"Of course."

"Do you not find me attractive?"

He shifted uncomfortably because it was a question he was not expecting to be asked.

After a bit of silence, he finally answered her by saying, "I very much do."

"Can I ask why you did not try to make love to me?"

He blushed heavily. The thought did cross his mind, but he was just so tired.

Deciding to be honest with her he replied, "I thought about it, but I was very tired from yesterday and fighting that I fell asleep. Also, if I'm honest I don't think it's very honorable for us to do that while not being married."

Marah shifted her body against his, a move that made him quite excited physically.

After a bit of uncomfortable silence of them sitting there near naked and pressed against each other she asked, "Do you think you might reconsider and still marry me if we can find a resolution to my problem?"

He once again shifted underneath her. It was quite a shock when she told him the truth, to the point that he considered walking away and ignoring her pleas for help. He was glad that he did not abandon her since it was clear this task was too much for her and he did care about her quite a bit. He just was unsure how he felt or what he would do. He reached out and grabbed her left shoulder with his hand. It was soft and warm, exactly how he daydreamed many times that it would be. Rone was amazed just how much she felt like a normal human.

"I'm still in shock of just how much you feel, look, and seem like a normal human just like me."

"Because when I transmogrify myself into a human, I am a human. As fully as human as you and any other. I'll be an excellent wife and provide you many children as my whole life since I was adopted by Uncle Gerrard had been to train to do that."

He nodded at her before answered, "I don't know."

She solemnly nodded at him before saying, "Its more than I probably deserve to have you at least unsure. I don't know if this matters, but I do love you deeply."

Not sure how to answer her, he said nothing.

"I suppose we should get going." She stated.

"We've got one more night before we should make it there. Hopefully we don't run into any problems, but we'll deal with whatever happens when it happens."

He spied a little closer at her naked torso as she shifted to move away from him to put her clothing on. It was quite a pleasant view and exactly what he imagined it would be. She was quite fit, and he almost regretted not taking up her offer for intimacy. While he knew the reality of what she was, he still found her very attractive, and he had to admit her personality was very pleasant to be around.

"Marah."

"Yes?" she asked as she turned her head to face him.

Rone sat up quickly and then kissed her. She responded to his kiss eagerly.

After breaking their kiss Rone said, "Already, let's go."

Marah flushed lightly at him and then stood up. Rone pulled himself off the ground. The injury on his back was feeling a little tender but it was nothing he could not handle. He checked the scratch on his arm and saw that it was healing nicely. He slipped on his spare tunic and then collected up his furs. After they both took a moment to use the restroom, they headed off. It was going to be a long day of walking and towards the end of the day they would have to start with some rough climbing. The only good news was that this mountain was the smaller one with much less rough terrain than the other peaks of the mountain range. Rone took a moment to look behind them as they began walking. They were still deep in the small forest that set along the side of this mountain, and he could not see anyone following them. They walked along quietly for some time before the forest broke out of sight and the first of the small ridges they would need to climb came into view.

Tired of the silence and wanting conversation he asked, "You mentioned that you trained to be a wife and have children earlier. What all did your aunt teach you?"

"Cooking, cleaning, sewing, and many times I got to act as a nursemaid for small children in the village."

"Why do you work as a seamstress?"

"I love it. For some reason I find making new things and fixing old things very relaxing."

Remembering how she always seemed to be wearing a new design every time he saw her, he asked, "Do you make all of your dresses?"

Giggling at him she answered, "Yes, and if you decide to marry me, expect to have to purchase a lot of materials. Making new designs is my favorite hobby."

"Have you ever considered selling your designs?"

She looked thoughtful for a moment as though the idea had never crossed her mind. She shook her head at him. Rone felt that the designs that she was wearing would have been very popular with the wealthiest members of town, maybe even to the point that they could be valuable.

He told her, "You should consider it. I feel as though you always wear such pretty dresses, and they would be popular if you sold them."

"Thank you for your kind words. Maybe if I find myself settled in town, I might just take up your idea."

Giving out a light chuckle, he took her clear hint. She wanted him to ignore the fact that she was a dragon who could become a human and still marry her. Initially he was repulsed by the reality of what she was. As he spent time with her, he had moved to being of two minds on the subject. After seeing her topless he was even more physically attracted to her than he had been beforehand. She was quite slender and fit.

Since it popped into his head earlier and he was curious about it he asked, "Can you control how you look and how your body is shaped?"

Shaking her head, she answered, "It's an odd thing. All I do is imagine that I'm a human and this is what I look like. The first time I did it, I was a tiny hatchling, and I became a small girl with orange hair. I grew up into what you're seeing now in the same manner every other human grows up. I'll continue to age as humans until I either go back to being a dragon or die."

"What happens if you die as a human?"

"I die as a human and my body stays as a human. I've been told that if I become sick with old age I need to sneak off and change back into my original form because if I die, that's it."

Rone nodded. He had not realized how precarious the situation could be. If they died as humans, they die. A sad fate probably for a species that can live for two thousand years.

"Why would you risk it? It seems like cutting your life short is a bad idea."

She grinned at him before answered, "Did you like how it felt when my breasts were pressing against you?"

He flushed lightly before nodding.

"It's an experience we can't experience as dragons. Our skin is light with feeling compared to humans. We don't experience physicality like humans. The physical touch of humans is as emotional as it is physical. It feels sooooo good. Goodness, I swear I could have dissolved into you. I've never felt anything like the sexual tension as we laid there near naked."

It did feel good to Rone. He simply nodded.

"Also, we've learned so much about technology and creativity from humans. Humans are not the strongest, wisest, nor most intelligent race. Yet, they've advanced further than any other race because of their creativity. We've become more like you than our fellow dragons and I think if we were forced to choose either to side with dragons or humans, we'd choose humans."

Based on what she was saying and what he knew about the other dragons, he could not blame her kind for not wanting to associate with other dragons.

He then asked, "Why can't you fly?"

"I'm too young. It usually takes fifty to one hundred years before our bodies can develop physically strong enough to fly."

Once again, he nodded. He suspected that he probably now knew more about dragons than anyone else in the kingdom. It suddenly hit him that the General, her aunt, or maybe her cousins might all be dragons.

He was curious so he asked, "Are your whole family dragons too?"

She shook her head before responding, "Only Uncle Gerrard. Auntie was born a human and he told her the truth. My cousins are humans like you."

"Your aunt knew and still married him?"

"Uncle Gerrard is amazing, and I guess many of our spouses find out and not only accept our kind but some even like it. I guess having a being that has lived for hundreds of years choose you over other humans makes some feel special or unique."

He sullenly nodded. The idea that the General was a dragon like Marah was surprising based on his long loyal career for the kingdom.

Pressing for more information he asked, "Is your aunt his first?"

"No. Uncle Gerrard is one of the oldest members of our race and he's a member of the Council of Orange."

"Council of Orange?"

"Our oldest and wisest members who guide and train all newest members of our race."

"Makes sense."

"They've taught me all that I know." She stated.

They arrived at a ridge that they needed to climb up. He knelt to allow her to use him as a base to climb up. He had to admit to feeling more than a little dirty since every time he helped her climb, he was able to put his hands on her in what would be an inappropriate manner if not necessary for the task at hand. Using his right hand, he grabbed hold of her rear and pushed upwards so she was able to climb up the ridge. He passed up his pack to her and then climbed up the ridge. It was a short easy climb. Once he got up he took the pack from her. Suddenly there was a loud wailing war cry. Rone spun towards the direction to see two orcs barrel directly at him. He dropped his pack and moved to draw his sword. Marah screamed out in fear. Before Rone could get his sword out, the two orcs collided with him and knocked him backwards off the side of the small ridge where he had climbed up. The impact of the landing caused a sharp amount of pain and then everything went black.

Chapter 21

Rone groaned out in pain as he opened his eyes. He was lying on the ground where he fell and his back called out in pain. His vision was very blurry at first but slowly recovered. The orcs who attacked must have thought him dead because they left him alone. Almost immediately he panicked when he realized that Marah was with them. Rone quickly jumped to his feet and looked around. It took him a moment to find his sword, which had fallen out of his hand and landed on the ground. Rone slipped it back into his sheath. He climbed up back onto the ridge, making sure to peek up cautiously to make sure the orcs were not waiting for him. Marah and the orcs were completely gone, and his pack was still sitting where he dropped it. Orcs were known to capture people and then eat them. They especially loved women and children. Rone had to hurry because he knew the nearest orc village was over a day away. That meant the orcs would likely have to camp at night so he would eventually catch them. He grabbed his pack and slipped it on before starting to look for indications of where they went.

"There!" Rone stated firmly to himself.

He spotted a rough scrabble where clearly Marah was pulled away while fighting. He then saw a dragging point. No doubt they dragged her away in that direction. Rone began to walk as fast as he could. It would not be wise to run as it would make a lot of noise. It was almost lunch time, so Rone pulled out some dried meat to eat while he kept walking. It was highly important to keep pushing if he wanted to catch up with the orcs. They moved at a slower pace than a motivated soldier, but they walked much faster than Marah could probably handle. No doubt she was struggling to keep up with them. He just hoped that she was okay. Rone spent the whole walk very concerned for her. Even though he knew that she was actually a dragon who could become a human, he still cared about her. The indication of where the orcs were headed was quite clear. They were heading to the village he knew about to the west and down the slope some. Chasing them down was going to slow down their overall progress if he were able to save her. He thought about the attack. It was only two orcs, and his best guess was that they were part of a small scouting party. Orcs tended to send scouting parties in groups of three to five so if he caught up with them either he was going to have to sneak into their camp when they stopped for the night, or he would have to ambush them to take out as many as he could. He was a very skilled and experienced fighter but the more orcs they had, the harder it would be for him to succeed in freeing her. His brisk pace worked as it got closer to sunset, he spotted the orcs that he was following. The lead orc had Marah's hands chained and was dragging her. She was a little rough looking as her dress sleeve on her right arm was torn off and he could see as she half walked, and half dragged behind the lead orc that she had a huge bruise on the side of her face where one of the orcs must have hit her. He was very angry seeing that the brutes had hit her. Rone decided to get a full measure of their numbers before moving. Watching and listening carefully, he spotted four orcs. The lead orc was dragging Marah and the other three were moving in a wide formation at enough distance to cover maximum ground but where they could still see each other. He decided to take out the furthest one while they were moving and then try to deal with the others one by one if possible. To keep fast movement, Rone stopped to get some distance before he removed his pack and set it down. He would come back later if he succeeded in freeing Marah.

Drawing his sword, he whispered reassurance to himself, "I will win."

When he first joined the military, he was told many times confidence was the key to success and sometimes mental reinforcement of success would help greatly. He moved quickly to catch up with the orcs, who were still slowly slogging along. Marah's slow pace was making it possible for him to catch up easily. After reaffirming that it was indeed only four orcs, Rone made his way to the largest orc on their right flank. Orcs were not stealthy at all. In fact, they made so much noise that they were easy to sneak up on, especially if they did not realize they were under attack. Rone knew that he had to incapacitate the orc so it could not warn the others. It would have to be a throat slash followed by a finishing stab. A grizzly task. Rone made his way up to his target. It was lumbering along slowly while grunting and shifting its weight. As he readied his attack, he realized that he was upwind. Right then the orc spun from his smell. Panicking from losing the initial moment of surprise, Rone quickly stabbed the brute right in the soft spot where its neck met its chest. He made sure to roughly lift upwards to prevent it from making noise to warn the others. Dark green blood spewed out of the brute and a soft whistling noise exited the wound. Rone quickly slashed to the right to cut its main arteries and cause it to heavily bleed. The brute tried to swing at him but the stun of Rone's attack must have slowed it greatly. Rone simply took a few steps backwards and the beast fell to the ground. It made a loud enough thump to attract the others, which Rone responded to by stepping behind a nearby tree.

He heard one of the orcs grunt out, "Grumane agh usht?"

Rone never could understand their crude language, but he knew when they were inquiring about their now missing comrade. Making sure to keep himself hidden behind a tree, Rone waited for the next orc to approach them. It must have found the body of the first he attacked because it bellowed out a warning. The other orc began walking towards their now-dead companion. Wanting to find a distraction, Rone looked around. He spotted a branch that looked small enough he could throw but heavy enough to make a lot of noise when landing so he picked it up. As the two orcs were close enough he could hear them saying something about the dead body, Rone threw the stick as hard as he could to the right before sidestepping slightly to his left of the tree. As the tree landed, he saw the two orcs in front of him look towards it. It was a perfect distraction so he lashed out with his sword and slashed the first of the two orcs across its neck. It bellowed and dropped its crude stone club before grabbing its neck. Rone took advantage of the damage to kick it to the ground. The other orc faced him and snarled before hefting its club.

It snarled out in a crude and broken common, "Die omie."

Rone was briefly stunned by the fact it could speak in his language. It made him seriously reconsider everything he thought about orcs and planned to report this to his superiors, if he survived this. His stun was immediately removed when the orc charged directly at him. Since orcs tended to be bigger and stronger, Rone knew that he could not engage it directly but would have to use his superior speed and swordsmanship to win. The orc's club came flying first, which Rone sidestepped to avoid while lashing out at the orc's side. It dodged his swing and stopped running before spinning and swinging wildly again. Rone ducked the swing only to be surprised by the orc diving right at him while he was crouching. Having no other choice, Rone rolled to his left to avoid the orc. After rolling to get enough of a distance, he spun around and stood up. The orc rose from his feet. From the corner of Rone's eye, he could see the other orc who had Marah by a chain around her wrists had pulled her closer and was watching the fight closely. The orc charged at Rone again, swinging his club wildly. Moving to his side, Rone lashed out carefully with his sword and cut into the side of the orc charging him. It was a nice masterstroke and helped Rone realize how he would have to fight the creature. It spun around and held its side with its free hand before releasing his hand and examining the blood coming from the wound. It snarled once again before charging once again. Rone did not expect it to fall for the same move so this time he dove away from the creature. As it circled around him, he continued to evade and avoid the creature. Suddenly, Rone was hit with an inspiration to continue dodging for a while to build the creature's frustration and once it became mad, he would change movement and aggressively attack. He continued dodging and moving away from it, which seemed to anger it more and more. Finally, Rone was confident that it was time to end this fight so when the orc charged again he feinted that he was about to dodge but then aggressively charged forward looking to strike right in the orc's chest. The move caught the orc off guard and before it could react, Rone's sword stabbed right in the middle of the orc's chest. It began to fall on Rone but he rolled with its body to hit the ground. He turned and pulled his sword out of its chest. The other orc that was holding Marah hostage raised its crude and poorly made metal sword towards her neck. It snorted at him as he approached while bringing its sword closer to Marah. He thought that Marah would be scared but she must have adjusted to being in a dire position. Rone's mind tossed wildly trying to come up with a plan to save her.

As he squared to a battle pose Marah told him, "In three."

It was a command to attack, which he was surprised to have her say. He clenched his sword in his hand while nodding.

"3."

The orc grunted and shifted while bringing his sword a little closer to her neck. It grunted out something in its language, which based on its body language was a threat.

"2."

Rone took a deep breath and got ready for the command.

"1." Marah called out before a bright light suddenly flashed and Marah disappeared initially before Rone spotted her as a small orange scaled lizard, he mentally corrected himself, as a dragon.

The orc's facial expression shifted to a look of confusion. Marah spun as a dragon and bit into the right thigh of the orc. Rone took advantage of the moment as the orc bellowed out in pain to dive forward with his sword aimed right at the orc's chest. His sword struck true as the orc slowly began to try and respond to. It was too late as his sword stabbed right into its chest and Rone collided with force into it to get it away from Marah. The orc scrabbled for a moment to try and fight him off but it was not successful as Rone landed on it. The orc's breathing was gargling in blood, which spewed out of its mouth and chest. He stood up over it and withdrew his sword and then wiped the blood off his sword on the orc's crude cloth tunic. As he turned away from the creature, he saw Marah as a human standing there looking right at him. She ran into his arms and hugged him while sobbing loudly. He held her in his arms.

"Thank you for saving me." She called out between sobs.

Chapter 22

Rone released her and then said, "We better get out of here just in case someone comes looking for this scouting party."

Marah nodded at him. He took her by the hand and guided her to his waiting pack. Once he put it on, they headed off back towards their destination. The sun was still up but it would not be long until it was night time. He wanted to get as much distance as he could and maybe settle for the night against a ridgeline so that they would be much less likely to be spotted with only one direction to approach them.

As they got a little distance from the bodies of the orcs Marah said, "I'm relieved that you live. I was very worried about what happened to you when the brutes knocked you off the ledge."

"I got knocked out but no other real damage. Thankfully the fall wasn't that far. I guess they thought I was dead."

"You're right. I heard them say that they wanted to check but the leader insisted that they take me to the chieftain."

Raising an eyebrow at her, he asked, "How did you understand them? The kingdom has been trying to learn their language for a while now."

She flushed at him before stating, "Our kind are hyperpolyglots."

"I have no idea what that means." Rone told her.

"Oh sorry. We have a natural and almost magical ability to learn, understand, and use new languages quickly. I was told it was because of our ability to transmogrify. Speaking of which, I hope you didn't mind me changing back to my dragon form. It seemed like the only way to get away from the beast."

Rone chuckled as he commented, "It was perfect. I bet that orc didn't know what hit him."

She giggled at him before sullenly stating, "I don't like reminding you of it but it was the only thing I think of to do. They tell me that our kind tends to be much more intelligent than other races, something that is passed on to any children we have."

"Being a hyperpolyglot?"

"No, intelligence."

"Henri didn't seem that intelligent, he barely spoke."

Marah laughed heartily while grabbing a hold of his arm.

Once she calmed down from laughing she told Rone, "He's very smart and really quite kind. I think he just is a little anti-social. My uncle is having a lot of trouble finding him a wife because he's so dang picky and doesn't like being in groups."

"I guess that's fair. One of my brothers is a loner. We had to force him to marry a young lady who was very outgoing to make up for his lack of social skills."

Marah looked thoughtful as they walked. She still was holding his arm. When she first had told him the truth about her, he would have been repulsed by her being this close. At this point he did not mind at all.

She then asked, "Maybe I should mention that to Uncle Gerrard?"

"I'd suggest it. Turned out to be a perfect match as she gets to be a social flower and my brother can hide in a corner."

They finally approached a ledge that had a deep enough cut into the side of the mountain to allow them to camp without being exposed to the environment. It would be a perfect spot to stop for the night. The sun was setting so he figured they both could use a night's rest. Tomorrow they should make it to the top part of the mountain.

He turned and announced, "We'll camp here tonight."

"Okay."

He took a moment to clear out the rocks and branches in a spot that was flat enough for them to lay on. Once he had the area ready, he spread out the large piece of fur and then set his pack

153

down before taking off his boots. Rone set the second large fur aside for later when it got colder. Marah took her boots off as well after she sat down. He opened up the pack and offered her some dried food.

"Thank you."

He nodded at her and then took a moment to eat his food. It was quite bland after a few days of eating the same thing but he was happy to have something to eat since it had been quite a rough day. The fact that she was able to become a small dragon helped greatly at that one key point. As he ate his food he wondered if her mentioning how the children of her kind born with humans would be more intelligent than normal humans was an attempt to sell herself to him. He had to admit that it would be advantageous for any children he might have to be smarter than normal, especially since he really wanted to see his children successful beyond anything he could do. Once he finished eating he decided to take off his sweaty tunic so he could dry both the tunic and himself off. He could only imagine that the pair of them stunk badly. He set his tunic on the top of his pack and then sat decided to sprawl out on the ground. Marah was watching him closely. Once he laid down, she stood back up and then slowly removed her dress and then her chest undergarment. It left her only wearing her undergarments on her lower body, a bloomer style pair of pants. She then walked up to him and sat down directly on his hips while facing him. He was immediately aroused but said nothing because he was shocked by her boldness. Reaching out with her right hand, she took his left hand and placed it right on her chest over where her heart would be. His hand covered a good amount of her chest and her left breast. It was the first time that he had touched a woman's breast and he loved the soft, but firm feel of it. She kept her hand holding his hand in place on her chest. He found the thousands of freckles on her skin nice to look at. It gave her skin a unique look to it.

"I owe my whole life to you Rone. I'd have died for certain if you didn't come back to me. The brutes said that I looked like I would be very soft and tender tasting. I'm appalled that they apparently eat humans."

"They do."

She stared deeply into his eyes as she said to him, "I'll either have you or I'll have none. I'm yours to do with as you please."

Rone was very unsure how to respond to her. He found her very attractive, but he still was very unsure about being with her based on what she really was.

Deciding to be honest he told her, "I can't deny my physical attraction to you but I'm still very concerned about everything."

Marah nodded at him but did not move his hand at all as she said, "I understand."

While letting go of his hand, she leaned forward and then outright laid right on top of him. Her chest was pushed into his and her head was settled next to his while facing towards him.

In a sultry tone she whispered, "I can feel something telling me that you want me."

Rolling to his left side, with her chest still pushed into him, she then said softly, "I'll be here all night either way."

Moving his left arm up and onto her back he struggled to keep control of himself. A very large part of him wanted her badly but he had to maintain his honor. It took him almost an hour to fall asleep.

* * * * *

Rone woke the next morning to the feeling of Marah's hand slowly moving up and down his torso. She was clearly enjoying both the bare skin contact and his fit form.

"Good morning." She said when he moved his head.

"Hello. Did you rest well?"

She looked right into his eyes and answered, "Not as well as I wanted but I feel refreshed."

Rone chuckled because she clearly was attempting to seduce him. It took every bit of his will to hold back. Even lying there with her, he deeply desired her. He would hold for his honor as his father had told him many times that a man should hold nothing over his honor. A very serious part of him had gone from revulsion about her reality to not sure if it mattered. He wondered what his father would have thought of all of this.

Shrugging off his thoughts, he said, "We should probably get going, we're a little over half a day away from the peak."

Marah rolled back on top of him before bringing her lips to his to give him a kiss.

She then sat on his lap before saying. "I'm looking forward to returning home. I pray they have a solution to my problem so I can return back to living with humans, hopefully not alone."

"I hear you. I'm intrigued by your home and I look forward to seeing it."

She grinned at him before pulling herself off his hips.

As she slipped on her dress she stated, "I need to go to the bathroom, I'll be right back."

"Okay."

As she walked away, he sat up. They had a bit of a walk still so he got up and cleaned up their small campsite by putting everything away and getting dressed. Once she returned they headed off. Since the area moving up was too steep they had to circle around and then work their way up. The incline was slowly getting steeper so Rone took the lead so that he could help pull her up as she struggled with the rough terrain. As he made it up to the next short piece of rough terrain. It came up to his waist, an easy hop up.

He instructed, "Let me climb up and then I'll help you up."

She nodded at him. Rone pulled off his pack and set it down. After hopping up, he turned around to accept his pack from Marah. Once she handed it to him, he slipped it on and then offered both of his hands to help her up. She took his hands and then he gently pulled her up. Once she was firmly on the ground he turned around. His jaw almost hit the floor when he turned around to find seven goblins staring at him with crude sticks in their hands. Usually goblins did not go this far up into the mountains so he was more than a little surprised to see them. As he moved to grab his sword to fend off the creatures someone from behind pulled his sword out of the sheath. Rone spun around to see what happened only to see the hideous face of an orc. It snarled at him and gestured with his sword to turn around. Rone blinked while very confused. After a few moments he realized that the orc was wearing Marah's cloak and her dress. It was Marah! She had turned into an orc.

Marah the orc grunted out, "Gurnlush okg yunnuli!"

He spun around to look at the goblins. Their facial expressions shifted from initial shock of seeing Rone to sudden fear.

As an orc Marah spoke again, "Hgunn fabil musni!"

Her voice was course and clearly very aggressive. He was very curious what she was telling them. Whatever it was worked perfectly because the seven goblins spun on their heels and ran away. Once the goblins were out of sight Rone began to turn around. He saw a pop of bright light and then once he finished turning around Marah was standing there. She was holding his sword in one hand and her other hand was holding her very torn dress in another.

She blushed heavily before saying, "Sorry, I was taught that goblins were deathly afraid of orcs so I took a chance to scare them off so you wouldn't have to fight them."

He chuckled before commented, "It seems to have worked perfectly. What in the world did you tell them?"

"That you're my prisoner and I would skin them alive."

"Kind words."

Marah laughed before stating, "And now my dress is ruined."

"I see this."

"There wasn't time to loosen it and orcs are so much bigger than humans."

"I've got a few longer pieces of cloth, do you want to use them to at least tie it in place so you're not running around near naked?"

"Yes please."

He set his pack down and started digging in it.

She wistfully commented, "I'd prefer to keep my nudity between us."

Rone laughed.

Chapter 23

Once they got Marah's dress tied together enough to keep her from ending up nearly naked, they started walking again. Rone found that the air was starting to get a little lighter as they kept moving. They had to stop several times to climb up small ledges and rocky formations. He was quite happy that these dragons put their home on a smaller and less rough mountain than the other options in this mountain range. The weather was quite lovely but looking back at Marah he noticed that the sun had done a number on her skin. She was no longer a pale white color, but her skin had a reddish hue to it, most likely she ended up getting a sunburn from all the time outside.

As they walked along Marah commented, "It's harder to breath here."

"Indeed. Don't you remember it?"

She shook her head as she answered, "I was a hatching when they flew me down to an open field."

"Is that when you became human?"

"Well… They had me practice a few times before just taking me there. Uncle Gerrard was the one who brought me down and took me in to raise me as his own human daughter."

"Your kind lead an interesting life."

She chuckled as she commented, "Not really. I've spent a huge majority of my life as a human living exactly how you live. Most of our time when we aren't humans is just living in our home up here. We don't really explore much when we aren't human because a flying dragon tends to catch attention."

"That makes sense I suppose."

"Especially since we aren't really much in a fight, especially compared to other dragons."

Wanting to know more he asked, "Does it hurt?"

"What?"

"When you transmogrify?"

"It tingles a little bit but otherwise nothing. I think the most unusual part about it is the difference between the races. I didn't really know about it until just now. Being an orc was very uncomfortable."

Rone chuckled because he had no doubt that being an orc was likely not fun.

"Also… I could tell by your facial expression when you first saw me, it was quite unattractive to look at."

Giving a shrug he stated, "It got the job done."

As he pulled her up a small ledge while holding her hand she stated, "I much prefer how you looked at me last night before we went to sleep."

She was talking about when she was sitting on his lap with no top on. He could only imagine his facial expression probably gave away his physical desire for her. Letting go of her hand as she was fully on the ledge, he just nodded. They continued walking as they slowly worked their way up the side of the mountain. It was about midday when he thought that he might have finally spotted what they were looking for. Up against the mountainside was a cave that looked like it was neatly carved into the mountain.

Pointing at the cave he asked, "Is that it?"

Marah answered, "Yes. I barely remember what it looks like."

"Do you think that maybe they took you away too young if you can barely remember it?"

Marah shrugged before answering, "Living with humans as a human is more who we are now than living here."

Rone said nothing as he worked his way through the rough terrain. He could see the cave clearly and he could have sworn he saw someone in the shadow looking at them. Marah appeared to be struggling through the large rocks strewn around them, so he took her hand to help her.

As they got close to the cave opening, she commented, "I'm a little nervous. I haven't been here in so long and I wonder how they'll react to me bringing this problem to their door."

While continuing helping her along he responded, "I'm sure once they find out what happened they'll be glad you came here instead of staying with the Kingdom's mages."

"I hope so." She stated.

They finally made it up the last small slope and as they approached the door, an elderly man hobbled out. He was a little bit shorter than Rone with long silver hair that was tied into a loose tail behind his back. With light brown eyes just like Marah, his skin was wrinkled heavily. The man was wearing simple blue tunic and brown trousers. He was using a wooden cane to assist in walking.

Before either he or Marah could speak, the man said, "I'm surprised to find Marazuanila and a young man at my door."

Rone guessed that her actual name must have been Marazuanila since the man was looking at her.

She curtsied deeply and said, "Elder Drunarazil, I have come across a serious problem that I need aid in dealing with."

"Come inside. The both of you look as though you've been through quite a bit."

Rone nodded at him. It was not exactly an easy journey, but they made it.

"Yes sir." Marah replied as she followed him when he started to slowly walk back through the cave opening.

Being interested in what was in the cave, Rone hurried to follow them. The cave entrance was indeed manually made as the walls were smooth. It continued for a little while before he spotted what appeared to be light coming from ahead. As they made it through the cave he was completely stunned. The interior of the mountain had been carved into a wide-open area with a few high stone columns that seemed to be carved as well into the mountain that acted as reinforcement of the cave. Within the cave was a small village! Marah's people had carved out a cave into the mountain and built proper buildings within it.

As they entered the outskirts of the village the elderly man turned to them and stated, "Marazuanila take your friend to the men's sauna so he can clean up. Once you both have cleaned up, come, and see me at the village square. I'll call the elders who are here so we can discuss your problem."

Marah again curtsied to him before saying, "Yes Elder."

As the man started to hobble away Marah turned to him and said, "Please follow me. I think I remember where the men's sauna is."

Once they moved a little bit away from the old man, Rone asked, "Marazuanila?"

She blushed heavily before answering, "That is my real name. I go by Marah because I think it sounds prettier."

Rone said nothing and nodded. He agreed that Marah was prettier, along with easier to say.

Stopping in front of a building, Marah stated, "Here you go. Take some time to relax and bathe. There should be some extra clothing for you to change into as well and we'll meet here in about forty minutes, okay?"

"That sounds good."

Marah paused for a moment looking thoughtfully at him before walking off. He wondered what she was thinking about. Shrugging it off, he entered the building. It was a well-built wooden building made with thick planks and painted a light brown color. The flooring itself was highly polished dark wood and he saw right away when he stepped inside that it was only two areas. The smaller entry area had a long row of benches and shelves with towels, soaps, and a bunch of clothing. Everything from light green to dark black tunics sat on the shelves. Rone took off his pack and set it down. Stripping off his clothes, he grabbed a large towel. He also spotted some matching trousers of various colors. Rone grabbed a dark blue tunic and pair of black trousers since he always liked dark colors on him. He then picked up a bar of soap and headed into the second room. Immediately, the heat

162

of the room struck him. Along the back wall, he spotted a small stone furnace with several buckets. That furnace is where the heat was coming from. He guessed each of the buckets had hot water in them. In the middle of the room were 5 large bathtubs, each with a long pipe and a spigot where the pipe was arched over it. It was a common sauna design throughout the Kingdom. Along the other wall were a few benches. Rone set his clothing, towel, and soap on one. Turning on the spigot for the middle, he walked over to the heated buckets and picked one up by the wooden handle. Rone dumped the bucket into the filling tub. After filling up the tub, he grabbed the soap he brought with him and then slid into the tub.

"That feels good." He grunted out.

It had been a rough few days between sleeping on the ground while filthy, fighting monsters, and Marah seemingly wanting to convince him physically to continue forward with the marriage. Doubts still lingered deep in his mind. There was no denying that the physical attraction between them was there. It took every bit of his power to keep himself from taking her both nights. Her personality was still very pleasant and if anything, the time alone with her on the mountainside only made him enjoy being around her more than he had. It all came down to the fact that she was not human. Well, she was not born a human. The door opened and Rone looked up to see the General enter with a town wrapped around his waist.

The General stated, "I'm glad to see Marah was right that you're here."

"Yes sir."

Rone watched as the General filled up the tub and then slipped into it.

After a bit of silence, the General commented, "Sounded like you've had a rough few days."

"The usual sir, orcs, goblins, and undead."

The General chuckled, "Based on what I heard you've also had to fend off a young woman as well."

Rone knew immediately that the General was talking about his niece. He must have had a conversation with her before coming to see him.

"Nothing I couldn't handle sir."

Giving out a light grunt the General asked, "So where do we go from here First Sergeant?"

Looking over at the General, Rone realized that the General was asking about his relationship with Marah, so he answered honestly, "I'm not sure sir."

The General rubbed his chin, which seemed like his favorite move.

He looked thoughtful for a moment and then asked, "What would have happened if you never found out about us?"

Rone frowned. It seemed like an odd question to ask since they were stuck where they were.

He answered, "I suppose I'd have married her, and we would have moved into the home I bought."

"Indeed. Likely, the both of you would have had a handful or more children and lived a long life together."

Giving a thoughtful nod, Rone was unsure what the General was getting at. Likely he was looking to convince Rone to move forward with the marriage.

Rone asked, "Why do your kind do it?"

The General laughed for a moment before asking, "Why not? We've got a unique ability and humans are amazing creatures. I've been every sentient race on this planet and only the humans I've found to be enjoyable to be and be around."

It was much like what Marah had told him. Rone said nothing and sat there quietly while rubbing the bar of soap over his skin. After a long time soaking in the tub, the General rose and started drying himself off. Once he finished drying off, he started to leave.

The General stopped at the door and then asked, "Young man, I've got the sense you're questioning if you should still marry my niece."

"I am."

"Something to think about in the form of two questions. Do you think she'll still be an excellent wife, and do you love her?"

Before Rone could respond the General left.

Chapter 24

After Rone finished bathing he got dressed and then collected his belongings. Once he was ready, he headed out the front door of the building. Marah was there waiting for him. She had changed into a nice light green dress. It was very basic looking compared to her many own dresses. Her hair was braided and the braid was wrapped into a bun on the back of her head. The heavy bruise from the orcs hitting her was still on her face but clearly someone had rubbed some lotion on it to help it heal. She smiled broadly when he came outside.

"Did you enjoy your bath?" She asked.

"Yes, thank you. It was a rough last few days and the hot water felt good."

Reaching out, Marah took his hand and then said, "Come with me."

He started to follow her and then commented, "This is quite impressive."

"Our home?"

"Yes."

"We learned it all from humans. Before we started living with humans, this was all just a large cave with nests. We've benefited greatly from living with humans."

"No doubt we've benefited from having men like the General serving us."

Marah nodded before adding, "Our kind have held important positions throughout the history of your Kingdom and we're just as loyal as any other. Many of us have died defending the Kingdom."

He nodded at her. Glancing down at her hand that was holding his, he noticed that she was still wearing the bracelet that he had given her for the engagement. He looked at her as she turned to look back at him, she gave him a beaming smile. She really was quite lovely when she was a human. He immediately realized that the General was right, she would indeed be an excellent wife. All that he had been through with her to get to this village in the mountain made him realize that he did still care very deeply about her. In fact, he probably cared more after it all. After their brief walk, they arrived at what was obviously the village square. He saw the elderly man who met them initially was there. The General was there, and he spotted maybe a dozen or so other people there. Rone had no doubt that all of them were dragons who became humans. One thing that he noticed was that all the younger ones seemed to have the same orange colored hair as Marah. All the older ones had silver colored hair. Standing next to the elderly man was an older looking woman. She had silver hair, light brown eyes, and light wrinkled skin. She was wearing a plain-looking red dress.

The elderly man was the first to speak, "So Marazuanila tell us what brings you home."

Rone stood still quietly and listened as Marah told them the whole tale of how she was almost discovered by the Kindgom's mages, Rone aiding her escape, and finally how Rone brought her up to the cave.

The elderly man looked thoughtful for a moment before turning to Rone and stating, "It sounds as though we owe you greatly for keeping young Marazuanila safe and returning her to us."

"It was my duty sir, honor demanded it."

"Yes, it did." The elderly stated.

Marah then asked, "What can we do? If I go back my ability to transmogrify is not strong enough to overcome inspection by their mages."

"A problem for certain. I suppose you will have little choice but to stay here until you're either old enough to mask yourself better or to be forgotten." The elderly man answered.

Rone frowned. He had hoped that they would have a better option. Marah frowned as well.

The elderly woman who was standing next to the man spoke up, "What about transfixation?"

"Transfixation?" Marah asked.

Rone had no idea what the word meant. He turned to look at the elderly man.

The man spoke, "It's too dangerous. She'll be stuck as a human."

He was mildly confused. Stuck as a human?

Marah asked excitedly, "But I'll not have to worry about the mages?"

The old man shook his head before continuing, "You won't but you'll be stuck as a human for"

She interrupted him, "If I'll be really human then, I'll do it."

Gerrard finally spoke, "Its dangerous niece. If something happens you won't be able to escape whatever fate lies in your path."

Marah turned to face him, "I don't care. Rone will protect me."

Rone was surprised by her statement. He was unsure he would be able to protect her for the long walk back, although he realized it would probably be safer to take a direct route to the east and then once they hit the roadway, they could walk north safely. It helped greatly that he knew where they were going and they did not need to avoid the Kingdom's men.

The elderly man looked over at Rone and then said, "She must have a naturally born human to bond with for the transfixation to work. Will you bond with her?"

Rone froze for a moment. If it were possible to make her permanently human, why was he hesitating? It would solve his one issue with her and allow them to wed.

168

After recovering he responded, "Yes."

Marah hugged him excitedly as she stated, "If I'm permanently human then we can be together."

He pulled away from her and then asked, "Is that what you want? To give up being a dragon and a long life just to be with me."

Marah looked up at him and right into his eyes before firmly telling him, "Yes. Life without you feels pointless to me. I'll take a short life with you than a long one without you."

Rone was touched that she felt that way about him. He reached out a hand and softly stroked her cheek, which she responded to by smiling at him.

Gesturing towards the elderly woman nearby, the man who seemed to be the leader of the dragons said, "Jasmidunin, go get the transfixation blade."

The woman looked hesitant for a moment before walking away. No one said a word as they stood waiting for her to return. Marah took his hand with hers. The woman returned after a brief wait and then passed a small wooden box to the elderly man.

"Thank you Jasmidunin." The man said.

He set the box down on a nearby table and opened it. Rone watched curiously. The box was unusually small to hold a blade within it. The man removed something from the box and as soon as he lifted his hands away from the box, Rone saw the blade. It was only a thin metal piece with what looked like sharp edges on the sides of it. The top and bottom of the blade were straight. The blade looked like it would have been long enough for a dagger at best and had not been finished. It seemed to not reflect light at all and was dark as obsidian. Using his other hand, the man took out a long piece of rope.

He turned to Marah and Rone as he declared, "Bring up a hand from each of you and press the blade flat between your hands."

As the man got closer to Rone, he saw that the dark metal seemed to have some sort of inscription on the blade in a language that he could not recognize nor read. He followed the man's instruction, and both pressed a hand with each other while holding the blade between their hands. The man wiggled the blade a little to have the excess length poke out of the bottom of where their palms met. Next, the elderly man took the rope and tied their hands together while pressed against the blade. His knot was tight enough that it almost was cutting the circulation to his hand.

Marah then asked, "Is there a spell or incantation that we must do?"

Chuckling, the elderly man answered, "The magic of transfixation is within the blade."

He reached out to the exposed part of the blade before commenting, "This might hurt a bit."

Before Rone could ask what he meant, the man quickly twisted the blade and then pulled downwards. The twisting motion he made forced the blade's sharpened edges to cut into Rone's palm and the pulling down of the blade dragged the cut along the full length of his palm.

"Ouch!" Marah yelled out.

Blood began to drip from the bottom of both his and Marah's palm where the blade was pulled from. Rone tried at first to pull his hand away, but it was firmly tied to Marah's.

"Wait." The elderly man instructed.

While his palm hurt, Rone followed the man's instruction. It did not take very long until the cut from the blade began to suddenly feel warm. He could tell immediately that Marah must have felt it because she looked at her hand and raised an eyebrow. The warmth began to increase and was starting to become hot. It got hotter and hotter to the point that it was starting to hurt. Rone struggled to manage the pain. He could tell that Marah felt it as fully as he did because her facial expression was one of pain. She started to cry out incoherently from the pain. Struggling to hold his bearing, Rone fell to his knees. Marah fell along with him. Suddenly, the heat completely disappeared. Marah's cheeks were wet where tears had been rolling down from her eyes.

"It is done." The elderly man announced.

Taking a moment, the elderly man reached over and slowly untied the rope from around their hands that were bound together.

"I don't feel different." Marah announced.

The elderly woman interjected, "Try transmogrifying to your natural form."

Marah paused for a moment and got a sudden look of concentration. She looked stunned as she seemed to be thinking quite hard about something.

Finally, she announced, "I can't."

"You can't what?" Rone asked.

"I can't transmogrify. No matter how hard I try." She answered.

The elderly man announced, "Of course you can't. A human cannot transmogrify. This is your form."

"I'm human?" Marah asked with a look of awe on her face.

"You are." The elderly woman stated.

She suddenly pushed herself into Rone's arms and started kissing him passionately. Rone kissed her back for a moment.

The elderly man gestured to another of the men who was there before stating, "Restock their supplies for the walk back to town."

"Yes sir." The man said before turning to Rone and instructing, "Please come with me."

Rone stood up and helped Marah to her feet before nodding at the man.

The General finally spoke, "Take care of her, her fate is now entwined with yours young man."

"I will." Rone stated firmly.

Marah wrapped both of her arms around his right arm and clung tightly to him as they followed the other man away from the village square.

Once they got a little distance away Marah told him, "I love you."

He gave her a grin as he answered, "I love you too. Let's go home."

Epilogue

Drunarazil watched as the couple walked away from them. Young Marazuanila was clearly excited about the results of the ritual and was clinging all over the human who was her mate.

Gerranumiquin asked, "Drunarazil you know that's not how the transfixation ritual works?"

Drunarazil chuckled before answering, "Of course but she doesn't know that."

Jasmidunin interjected, "I'm envious of her."

Turning to her Drunarazil raised an eyebrow and asked, "How so?"

Jasmidunin grinned at him before answering, "She thinks she'll forever be a human instead of just until her mate dies so she's going to experience her first in a way that humans experience love. It'll be sincerer and more passionate than anything we've ever felt."

Drunarazil had not thought of it that way. Living as humans was a wonderful experience every time that he had done so but nothing had been like his first. A blonde-haired woman named Maria. Just thinking about her and their children made him smile. She was a wonderful person and when she died, he cried about her loss for decades. It took almost two hundred years to recover enough to try it again. The foolish girl was likely to never recover when that human named Rone finally would die. Jasmidunin was right, it was going to be a special love.

Thank you

I would like to take time to thank God for life and my family, my passion for writing and fantasy/sci fi and our crazy imaginations! I would like to thank my beautiful wife Parneeta for being my continuing to push in writing. To my three kids, Shawn II, Spencer, and Astir. I love each of you. To my family and friends for being as such, even if you did not want to be. Thank you to Christian Neumann for the lovely artwork on the cover. Lastly, I would like to thank you, the reader. Without you, this is all pointless. I hope you enjoyed *Orange*.

About the Author

Born in Muskegon, MI and raised in Concord, CA, S.W. Gunn used his early experience as a roleplaying geek to expand upon his imagination. Unable to purchase the proper Dungeon and Dragons manuals at a young age, he developed his own roleplaying paper and pen game for himself and his friends to play. While living in Hawaii, he completed his Bachelor's in Art degree in History at Chaminade University of Honolulu. He is married to his lovely wife Parneeta and they have three wonderful children, Shawn (2nd), Spencer, and Astir. They live in Phoenix, AZ.

Other works by this Author:

The Heima Series:
Heima: The Ninth Kostir
Heima: Challenge to the Crown
Heima: Neinn

The Legenda Series:
Smuggler's Luck
Gift of Flight

Paladin Series:
The Thrill of Battle

Acciaccato
The Almighty Paw
The Priestess Princess
Angels of Evernal
Medusa
First Contact

Non-fiction Works:
Historical Journey through a Master's Degree
American Federalism: A Changing Political Philosophy

Made in the USA
Middletown, DE
22 August 2023

37181714R00106